As Rainey handed the tray up to him, their gazes met again.

Sheer beauty.

And it wasn't because of her lovely face, her gold-toned skin or the soft tumble of hair.

It was her spirit, shining through the smile she gave him.

His chest tightened, as it did the week before, when he'd first laid eyes on her. But inside, his heart melted.

Think, man. She's got a troubled history.

He knew that. Rainey's teenage years had been nothing but trouble, but in all his years on the force, he'd seen a lot of kids change their lives. Why not her? Why not now?

Was he willing to risk his son's well-being? He was a grown man. Aidan was a kid who'd already drawn the short straw on mothers once. Leave it alone.

Luke had to. He knew it.

But ignoring this attraction to Rainey was the last thing he wanted to do.

Books by Ruth Logan Herne

Love Inspired

RUTH LOGAN HERNE

Born into poverty, Ruth puts great stock in one of her favorite Ben Franklinisms: "Having been poor is no shame. Being ashamed of it is." With God-given appreciation for the amazing opportunities abounding in our land, Ruth finds simple gifts in the everyday blessings of smudge-faced small children, bright flowers, freshly baked goods, good friends, family, puppies and higher education. She believes a good woman should never fear dirt, snakes or spiders, all of which like to infest her aged farmhouse, necessitating a good pair of tongs for extracting the snakes, a flat-bottomed shoe for the spiders, and for the dirt…

Simply put, she's learned that some things aren't worth fretting about! If you laugh in the face of dust and love to talk about God, men, romance, great shoes and wonderful food, feel free to contact Ruth through her website at www.ruthloganherne.com.

The Lawman's Holiday Wish

Ruth Logan Herne

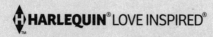

Recycling programs
for this product may
not exist in your area.

LOVE INSPIRED BOOKS

ISBN-13: 978-0-373-81736-8

THE LAWMAN'S HOLIDAY WISH

www.Harlequin.com

Printed in U.S.A.

He that is without sin among you,
let him cast the first stone.
—*John* 8:7

To my wonderful son Luke, a young man whose strength, grace, humor and brilliance has been a beacon to his parents. Luke, we're so very proud of you! Merry Christmas!

Acknowledgments

Huge thanks to my dear husband, Dave, for road-tripping with me to Chautauqua Lake and Jamestown, New York, the inspirational settings for the fictional "Kirkwood Lake." To Mandy and Beth for doing the same thing, and the laughter and fun we have on each trip. To the Pittsford Dairy, my model for a glass bottle dairy and bakery. To the migrant workers I've met over the years— men and women whose work ethic abounds under tough conditions. God bless you! To Nancy Turner and the crew at www.thisoldhorse.org in Hastings, Minnesota, for her wonderful advice on how to handle "Spirit's" role in this story. Nancy, you are an amazing woman with a great "spirit" of your own. Thank you so much for your help! It was invaluable. To Virginia Carmichael for her advice on Tres Leches cake! And a huge round of thanks to my daycare moms, whose encouragement and trust humbles me. I love youse guys.

Chapter One

Deputy Sheriff Luke Campbell aimed his cruiser for the Kirkwood Lake Elementary School with measured reluctance. A mandatory meeting with his five-year-old son's principal and teacher didn't bode well for him or the boy. It didn't take an early-education degree to tell Luke what he already knew. Aiden was quiet, withdrawn, uncertain, timid and refused to join activities.

Luke had hoped being in school would help, but this was the second phone call in three weeks regarding Aiden's issues. How much was real and how much exaggerated by a smart kid who knew how to evoke adult sympathy to the max?

Luke didn't have a clue.

Did he tend to make excuses for the boy?

Yes.

Did he have good reason?

Yes again, but unless he wanted to be a failure as

a parent, he had to find a way to bring Aiden around. The sooner the better.

He's five. Give him time.

Luke shoved the thought aside. He'd been telling himself that for nearly three years, since Aiden lost his mother. School was important, and getting along with other kids was invaluable, all the books said so. They called it "socialization."

Luke was the third of seven Campbells, three of whom were adopted. In the Campbell house, you either socialized quickly or got taught a lesson by your big brothers.

Luke's sweet mother had been praying for Aiden's situation to improve.

Luke used to pray. Back before he realized the improbability of a just and beneficent God. Because if God *did* exist, He'd messed up the job, and Luke knew that firsthand.

But if it made his mother feel better to pray, who was he to argue? Jenny Campbell was a great lady, a wonderful mom and grandma, and Luke loved and admired her. He'd leave the praying to her and her church friends.

An aging Camry darted into the school driveway ahead of him, then pulled to a quick, crooked stop in the mostly empty parking lot.

Luke angled into the spot alongside the other car and climbed out. He turned and locked gazes with the dark-haired woman staring at him, her un-adorned hands grasping the top of the car door.

Breathtaking beauty. Tall and slim. Scared to death.

You're in uniform, Einstein.

Of course. She thought he'd followed her into the school lot to issue a ticket, but she hadn't done anything wrong. The posted signs were school-in-session speed limits, and she hadn't exactly careened around the corner on two wheels.

But her face held more than concerned chagrin. It held fear, and the cop in him wondered why she feared police. He jerked his head toward the building as he walked that way. "You here for a meeting, too?"

Relief eased her jaw and the set of her shoulders. She nodded as she matched his stride. "Yes."

Vulnerable but tough; they were two red warning flags, despite the instant attraction. Luke stayed away from vulnerable women. Once burned, twice shy.

Tough women weren't his cup of tea, either.

His older brother Jack had scolded him the week before. Said he was afraid to shop around because he couldn't find June Cleaver.

Was Jack right?

Most likely. But this woman wasn't making eye contact with him, so the attraction must be one-sided.

Or she's hiding something.

And that was just one more reason to keep his distance. If he could get beyond the caramel skin. The past-her-shoulders, wavy dark hair. Eyes round and deep-toned. "You've got a kid here?"

"Two."

That surprised him. She looked young, mid-twenties. Too young to have two elementary school kids, at any rate. But maybe she wasn't too young. He might be feeling old before his time.

He stepped forward and swung the door wide for her.

She glanced up to thank him.

Time stopped.

So did she.

Her eyes, a blend of storm-cloud gray and milk-chocolate brown, were a shade he had no name for. Brows, thin and arched, framed long lashes that looked real. Her mouth, soft and full, was perfectly shaped....

No makeup.

Unusual. Didn't all beautiful women wear makeup these days?

She opened her mouth as if to speak, then stopped, pressed her lips together, turned and moved through the door. But that moment—seconds that felt like long, drawn-out minutes—assured him the electricity went both ways.

They walked down one hall side by side, turned right, then proceeded to the principal's office.

Mr. O'Mara stepped through his door. He nodded to Luke and sent a look of commiseration to the woman. "Rainey, I'm sorry, but you're late. Deputy Campbell's meeting is scheduled to start now. Can you wait here and we'll meet about the twins once we're done talking with Luke?"

Rainey.

Rainey Cabrera McKinney, the woman who'd done time years ago for a crime she didn't commit. A woman who'd skated the edge of the law too often as a kid. His friend Piper McKinney had been raising Rainey's twin daughters until Rainey returned to the family farm last month.

"Rainey wants to make amends," Piper had told him.

The word on the street, and the look on her face, said the whole making-amends thing wasn't going too well. Luke's mother had a saying: "Small-town folks have little to talk about, and drawn-out winters to do it."

With winter approaching, Piper McKinney's sister might be in for a long, hard haul.

Rainey nodded, stepped back and took a seat on the hand-crafted wooden bench outside the office. "It's no problem, Mr. O'Mara. I'll wait here."

Deep and poignant, her soft "Tex-Mex" voice complemented her looks, but that could be another strike against her. Kirkwood Lake was a great town, but with the summer recreational season over, people would have too much time on their hands. That could make things tough for the woman to his left. As if taking the fall for a dishonest friend and doing prison time wasn't rough enough.

But right now he had his own personal dragon to face. He stepped into the office, gave a brisk nod to Miss Patterson, Aiden's teacher, and took a seat. "About my son…"

Rainey drew a deep, calming breath.

The deputy had surprised her in the parking lot. She'd turned, seen his cruiser and frozen.

His look said he'd wondered why, but when the principal called her by name, she'd read awareness in the officer's eyes.

He knew who she was. What she'd done. And what she'd failed to do by leaving her daughters in others' care for three long years.

You have been cleansed, my daughter, clothed in the light. Grace has come upon you as the dewfall….

She loved that image. Silent, encompassing, peaceful.

Then why did her gut clench? Her thoughts ran rampant, wondering what the girls' teachers would say.

Rainey stared at the door, wishing her mother or sister could have come along. But they were shorthanded at their Western New York dairy today, and someone had to watch Sonya and Dorrie.

You won't have to worry about being shorthanded if your customer base keeps shrinking.

With Rainey's return, customers at the dairy had diminished, sales were down and profits eroding, all because Rainey had taken the helm a few weeks back.

Her mother brushed it off. Lucia McKinney embraced an "and this too shall pass" mentality. She believed things would work out in God's time, one way or another.

So did Piper.

Not Rainey. She hadn't come home to mess things up more thoroughly; she'd come back to make things right. Set the record straight. And reclaim her position as the twins' mother, a role she'd abdicated to keep them safe when a rogue cop threatened Rainey's freedom…and her baby daughters.

Old guilt pricked her new and growing faith. Her girls were having trouble in school.

Were they following her example? Were they incorrigible? Or were they just normal kids fighting change, as Piper and her mother insisted?

The murmur of voices in the room said the officer—Luke Campbell, she remembered—was being bombarded. Maybe they'd get it out of their systems with the big, strong deputy and go easy on her.

The door to the office opened.

Luke came out, looking none too happy.

Mr. O'Mara's expression wasn't any better.

The teacher looked aggrieved. None of this boded well for Rainey's time in the hot seat.

Luke waved her in. "Your turn in the line of fire, I believe."

"Luke, we—"

"Mr. O'Mara, I understand where you're coming from." Luke turned to face the principal, and from the clipped sound of his voice, he wasn't pleased with what had been said. "But I'm not letting anyone label Aiden at this point in his life. Yes, he has emotional issues. We're trying to fix that. But I'm not allowing him to be placed in a special education classroom because his teacher expects a kindergartner to instantly conform to a new situation."

"But—"

"We'll talk at conference time in November," Luke insisted, and Rainey had to admit the guy had a point. Maybe some five-year-olds could adjust quickly to a new setting and new people. But was it that big a deal if a kindergartner took a few weeks to settle in?

She wouldn't have thought so, but then she wasn't an example of stellar behavior. And her lack of experience put her maternal instincts into question.

The teacher's noncommittal face said she disagreed. Mr. O'Mara appeared caught in the middle, but he stepped back, defusing the situation. "We'll keep you apprised of Aiden's progress. Miss Patterson and I both thought you should be brought on board from the beginning. You know we don't make these recommendations lightly."

Luke faced the principal directly. "We didn't used to, Frank. But kids get pigeonholed more easily today than in the past, and I'd like a little more time for Aiden to adjust. He's not causing a problem, right?"

"No."

"It's hard to cause a problem when you do nothing," Miss Patterson replied. Her tone of voice was condescending and sanctimonious, as if she'd just been appointed the resident expert on five-year-olds.

That made Rainey suck in a deep breath.

Educated people intimidated her.

Yes, she'd gotten her associate's degree in veterinary technology while serving time. And she'd worked as a vet tech for three years outside Chicago. But a two-year degree didn't put her on equal footing with a licensed teacher who'd obtained her master's degree in early education.

Luke must have caught her apprehension from the corner of his eye, because he leveled a look at her, one that intimated they were in this together, and said, "I'll see you outside, Rainey."

The teacher's gaze sharpened.

Mr. O'Mara showed no reaction. He just waved to Luke and turned toward Rainey.

A second teacher stepped into the room—Mrs. Loughlin, Dorrie's teacher. Rainey knew her. She used to be a steady customer at the dairy store, and her kids had gone to school with Rainey and Piper. Would Rainey's past color the older woman's opinion? Should she consider sending the twins to the small Christian school over in Bemus Point, where her youthful indiscretions weren't so well-known?

She'd think about that later. Right now she needed to face these professionals and prove she was capable of mothering her girls in proper fashion.

She sat. Miss Patterson took a chair to her left, Mrs. Loughlin to her right. Frank completed the circle by drawing his chair forward. "Thank you for coming in, Rainey."

"I'm sorry I was late. I know how important it is for the girls to have a successful school experience from the beginning."

"Mmm-hmm." Miss Patterson's thin smile said she agreed. Her posture said she doubted Rainey's ability to ensure any such thing. "Sonya's a delight. A true treasure. So sweet, so endearing." Her insincere smile came with an incoming-missile warning attached.

Miss Patterson's brains might intimidate Rainey. Her veiled contempt didn't. "But?"

Mr. O'Mara frowned.

Mrs. Loughlin sat quietly, hands folded.

Miss Patterson leaned in, cool as a fish on ice at the Saturday marketplace. "She doesn't want to do anything without her sister."

"Identical twins are often very close."

"It makes things difficult," the teacher continued. "She stares at the door, willing it to open. She's distracted every time people go by in the hall. And she doesn't mix well with the other children."

"Is she disruptive?"

"No."

"Annoying others?"

"No. Just…off in her own little world."

"So she's having adjustment problems in a new setting, and with a whole new set of expectations from strangers. That sounds fairly normal for a five-year-old." Rainey might not be licensed to teach, but Sonya's difficulties didn't seem out of the ordinary for her first month in school.

"Rainey, I think that sums it up quite well," Mr. O'Mara said. His tone said he didn't find the child's prognosis worrisome. "And I think Sonya will do fine once she gets over her shyness and her fear. But I needed you to hear Miss Patterson's concerns firsthand."

"Which I appreciate, Mr. O'Mara. And now, what about Dorrie?" She turned to Mrs. Loughlin, and her hopes plummeted as she read the negative look on the older woman's face.

Mrs. Loughlin wasn't a bad person. Her son had wanted to date Rainey in high school and his mother had been against it. Rainey didn't blame her. Staying away from Rainey's crowd had been in his best interests.

Now she wished people could see the new and improved woman she'd become. She'd returned to Kirkwood Lake determined to set the record straight. What did she have to show for her first two months? She'd messed up her daughters and eroded the dairy's customer base, and with the all-important end-of-year sales approaching, she needed to find some way to fix things.

Fast.

"They may look alike, but Dorrie is quite different from her sister in many ways. I'm sure you've noticed that, Mrs. Loughlin."

The teacher listed Dorrie's negative attributes first, which raised the principal's brow. "She's tough, bossy, opinionated, and would take over the class in a heartbeat if I let her."

That sure sounded like Dorrie. Rainey met Mr. O'Mara's gaze. "And how is this being handled in school?"

Mrs. Loughlin cut in before he had a chance to respond. "I've tried cautions, both verbal and physical. You know, a hand on her shoulder, a warning to slow down and wait her turn. I've employed studious ignoring, quiet reminders, and I'm thinking of setting up a sticker program to see if that helps the situation."

"A sticker program?" Rainey repeated. "A reward program, you mean. Stickers for good behavior."

"A move like that can be beneficial to all concerned."

Rainey breathed deeply, considering.

They'd called her on the carpet because one girl was quiet and sad about being separated from her twin, while the other was being a rambunctious, noisy twit.

And they'd drawn Rainey in to let her know they wanted to do a sticker reward program to help encourage good behavior? Or to make the point that her kids were apples that hadn't fallen far from the tree?

Yes, the girls needed to behave. They needed to learn. But they were only three weeks into the year.

Luke's words came back to her. He'd said he'd readdress the issues at conference time in November if they still existed. Well, that sounded good to her. "I will be happy to do whatever it takes to reinforce their good behavior in school and at home. Their education is very important to us. And then we can meet again at their scheduled conference in November to reevaluate."

"Us?" Miss Patterson asked doubtfully. She exchanged a not-so-furtive look with Mrs. Loughlin, and in that moment, Rainey knew she'd never convince these women of her change of heart.

She cleared her throat, mustered a smile and

stood. "My family. The McKinneys. We'll work together to help the girls."

"Wonderful." Mr. O'Mara stood and extended his hand. "I knew we could count on you, Rainey."

His words blessed her. His countenance, too. And the flat look he leveled in the teachers' direction meant he wasn't thrilled with how the meeting had gone, but it wasn't Rainey's behavior that disturbed him.

It was theirs.

Rainey thanked them, pushed through the heavy, plate-glass door of his office and wound her way back to the front. Bottled energy surged forth now that the meeting was over.

Her heart raced. She had an urge to punch someone, but common sense drew her up short. She knew she'd changed. Others didn't, so she shouldn't blame them for living in the ashes of a past best forgotten.

And her heart tipped straight into warp factor when she stepped outside on this beautiful fall day and saw Luke Campbell waiting for her, just as he'd said.

Only she hadn't believed him. Or even thought of it again until just now, but there he was, heading her way. He raised a hand to his forehead, shading bright blue eyes from the glare of the late-afternoon sun. Short, blond hair edged his deputy's cap. Broad-shouldered, square-jawed, he looked like a modern-day Celtic warrior.

"You survived." He ambled forward, not appearing too happy. But something in his face—an expression that said he understood what she'd just endured and wanted to help—softened the rapid beat of her heart. The spike in her pulse. The knot of dread that formed in her gut every time someone peered at her and saw the old Rainey...

"Alive, but not unscathed."

The glint in his eyes said he reciprocated the feeling.

"You waited for me."

"I said I would." He flicked a glance at the school, reminding her of his promise inside. "And I'm a man of my word."

"Why did you wait?"

He fell into step alongside her. "I could tell Miss Patterson was spoiling for a fight. She'll go easy on me because her younger sister is married to my uncle. I was afraid she might take it out on you."

"Pretty unprofessional."

Luke took three long steps before answering. "She lost her parents this past year. I know she's been struggling. My aunt thought she should take a leave of absence, but she wouldn't hear of it. Keeping busy might be good for her, but I'm not sure it's in the best interests of her students."

What a conundrum. Still, the deputy was right. The kids should always come first. But who was Rainey to judge? She had a host of grave mistakes on her record already. She turned his way as they reached their cars. "We'll give her time."

The deputy didn't look convinced. "I don't offer a lot of leeway when I'm talking about my kid."

Add protective and loving to crazy good-looking and a pulse-stopping smile.

Add nothing. He's a cop. You're an ex-con. Even with your record expunged, you did time. And then you left your girls.

She had. She knew that. But she'd returned, determined to make things right. At the moment, she wasn't sure if her return was selfless or self-motivated but that was her personal dragon to slay. "Ex-cons don't get much leeway, either."

To his credit, he didn't pretend otherwise. "True."

"Life might not offer do-overs, but everyone deserves a second chance." She aimed her gaze up to his. "Don't they?"

His face said maybe. Maybe not. From a cop's perspective, his reluctance to agree made sense. From hers?

His reticence was another chunk in a well-built wall. A wall she needed to scale or break down, one brick at a time. She looked beyond him to the terraced village leading down to the water's edge. Yellowing foliage blocked the shoreline view. Once the leaves turned completely, they'd fall. The holiday season would be at hand, her first Thanksgiving and Christmas with her girls in years. That was enough, wasn't it?

Unless you shouldn't have come back at all. The insidious whisper crawled up from somewhere deep within. *The girls are struggling and your effect on the family business may prove disastrous. Who exactly are you helping by your presence in Kirkwood?*

Her hands went cool and clammy. A shiver that had nothing to do with the fall weather crept up her spine. "My decision to come home—to fix things—might be more a detriment than a help," she admitted. "And that's the reality I wake up to each morning these days." She turned and moved toward her mother's car, knowing her past limited her future, but those do-overs she talked about? The ones that weren't possible?

Oh, how she wished they were.

A detriment?

Impossible, thought Luke. Not with her face, her hair, those eyes, storm-cloud gray, deep and luminous. Eyes that held a constant mix of emotions. Her life held a blend of misdeeds and misfortune, sure, but everyone had a past, including him, and smart folks knew enough to let it be. Unfortunately, not everyone in town saw things that way.

The urge to protect and defend rose within him, but Luke sloughed it off. He'd loved a woman with issues once, and losing her had nearly killed him. It *had* killed his faith and a good share of his hope, at least until they'd found Aiden, unharmed. Hope had bloomed that day, within a cloud of sorrow.

Aiden came first, from that point forward. "I'd like to offer you a proposition. About our kids."

Rainey looked at him, confused, and Luke smiled. "Aiden loves your girls. I've been working overtime since you got back home, and with all the drama at the farm, I knew your family was crazy busy."

They had been fighting off an eminent domain petition put forth by the town supervisor. For a few weeks, tensions ran high, until the town ruled in favor of McKinney Farms. Still, Luke's words were only half-true. He'd avoided his friend's farm because Rainey was back. Coming face-to-face with a woman who'd abandoned her children didn't make his short list. Fate had decided otherwise today. "Aiden comes out of his shell when the twins are around."

"Okay…" She drew the word out, as if wondering where he was going. But she was willing to listen.

"I was thinking we could strategize together. Dorrie brings out the adventurer in Aiden when they play together. Aiden brings out the protector in Sonya. And together they help Dorrie think twice before getting into trouble. What if we set up a way to help them help us?"

"You mean playdates?

He shrugged lightly. "Beyond that. Like our own

little classes to help reinforce good behavior. Does that make sense to you?"

Rainey paused, thinking. "I can't give you an answer right off. First, because it sounds good and that means there's most likely a flaw we've overlooked."

He nodded, but the only flaw he saw was that being around Rainey could prove dangerous to his heart. Luckily, he believed in aspirin therapy and a good diet. Except for nachos on game days. And strawberry-rhubarb pie. He wasn't opposed to ice cream from McKinney's Dairy Store, either.

"Second, I don't wade into unknown waters. I think and pray, and that's stopped me from doing and saying a lot of stupid things as an adult. Including some of the thoughts that ran through my mind in that meeting." She frowned in the direction of the school.

Her honesty made him smile. "I concur."

"Third." She met his gaze. And while he read the uncertain shadows in her eyes, she proved she had them under control with her next words. "Getting involved with anyone isn't on my agenda, Luke. So if this is your version of a pickup line, you get a gold star for ingenuity. But I'm not interested."

Her eyes said the words weren't quite accurate. She *was* interested but didn't want to be.

Well. That made two of them.

Her firm stance said she wouldn't budge an inch.

And that made Luke wonder—for just a moment—
if he could convince her otherwise.

He let go of that thought instantly, but it came
back to haunt him after they agreed to talk later in
the week, and said their goodbyes.

The deal was good for both of them. And he
couldn't pretend that spending time with Rainey
would be punishment. Not with that face, that hair,
that voice.

He refocused his thoughts on the kids, three ras-
cals who needed time and space to establish their
roots. His mother believed good family roots allowed for great wings, and Luke was determined
Aiden should have both, even if he'd been reluctant
to follow through in the past. Maybe with Rainey's
girls around more often, the three of them could
attain more solid ground together.

Chapter Two

Rainey strode down the hall to Miss Patterson's room on Friday afternoon. Mr. O'Mara met her at the door. "I'm sorry we had to call you in, Rainey, but we've got a situation here."

Mr. O'Mara was the kind of principal that kept his cool. Today he looked exasperated. At her? At the twins? She didn't know. "How can I help?"

Her words softened his expression. "Come over here." He walked to a door on the far side of the empty room.

"Where are the kids?" She glanced around the classroom. Bright-toned fall leaves decorated a mural of trees on two walls. Alphabet squares took the place of fruit and nuts among the branches, an inviting way of introducing letters to small children. "Art class? Music?"

"We took them into the gym for playtime so they wouldn't witness adults pulling their hair out over the antics of two miscreants." Miss Patterson bit the words through tight teeth, looking none too pleased. Was it Rainey's presence or the twins' misbehavior that pushed her this far?

"Sonya and Dorrie, this is Mommy speaking. Come out of there. Now."

"Dorrie's not in there."

A deep voice rumbled from Rainey's left, and she didn't have to turn to see the deputy sheriff's broad chest and shaved chin, he was suddenly standing so close. Warmth emanated from his dark blue uniform shirt. His tie was crooked, as if he'd loosened it, unthinking. He was hatless right now, and his blond-brown hair curled slightly, even cut short. "Aiden and Sonya have locked themselves in the closet."

Rainey couldn't resist. "That's a pretty bold move for a couple of shy kids."

"But we'd prefer they embolden themselves in a socially acceptable manner," interjected Miss Patterson, unamused. "Rather than disrupt the entire afternoon lesson with this nonsense."

Luke shifted slightly. His shoulders rose. His chest broadened. To save them from the outburst she figured was coming, Rainey stretched out a hand. "Give me the key and I'll open the door."

Mr. O'Mara frowned. Miss Patterson looked suddenly guilt-stricken.

Luke's mouth dropped open as realization struck. "You don't have a key to this door?"

"It appears to be missing."

"Because I haven't needed to lock this closet ever." Miss Patterson's voice tightened. "Therefore there was no need for a key. Until today, that is."

"Have you called a locksmith? Doesn't the janitor have a master set of keys?"

Mr. O'Mara nodded. "We've called in a locksmith from Clearwater, but he can't get here for another hour. And for some reason, it appears that Mr. Gordon doesn't possess a key to this particular door, either."

"So you have a door in the kindergarten classroom that locks from the inside, but has no key?"

"As I said…" Miss Patterson drew herself up to her full five-foot-two-inch height, as if posturing would help the situation. "We haven't needed one—until today."

"That doesn't eliminate the negligence of not having one," Luke offered. His tone was mild, but tension rolled off him. "Right now my son is locked in a closet and we can't get him out. With Aiden's history…"

Rainey had no idea what Aiden's history was, but a giggle from the closet interrupted Luke.

A second giggle joined the first.

Clearly, the two children were more at peace with the situation than the four adults gathered around the door.

"Aiden Campbell, open that door. Now."

Silence reigned momentarily before being broken by another laugh.

Rainey nudged Luke with her elbow. When he turned, she swept his sheriff's attire a quick glance. "He's obviously in awe of the uniform. And your authority."

Luke sighed and eyed the hinges before shifting his attention to the principal. "Can we pop the hinges?"

Mr. O'Mara shook his head. "They appear slightly warped, so no. We can't."

More whispers and giggles from inside the closet weren't helping the situation, although Rainey was tempted to laugh right along with the two naughty kids. What did that say about her lack of parenting ability?

Miss Patterson's anxiety was sky-high, and Mr. O'Mara had gone from frustrated to angry with himself. "It's certainly a situation we'll rectify now that we've been made aware of it. The lack of key and the bad hinges. But in the meantime…" He cast a glance to the locked closet. "We have a problem."

"Call Dorrie in here," Luke advised.

Rainey turned, puzzled.

Mr. O'Mara seemed surprised at the request, as well. Miss Patterson rolled her eyes. "That's a big help."

"It could be." Luke's tight tone said Miss Patterson was skating on thin ice. His grim expression said he found the teacher's behavior unacceptable. "Dorrie's got a knack for dealing with these two, as odd as that might seem. Shall I get her?" he asked Mr. O'Mara.

The principal turned on his walkie-talkie. "I'll have her sent right over."

Moments later, Dorrie skipped into the room, one pigtail dangled low, half undone. The other still hung neatly in place with a perky purple ribbon. She looked happy, spunky and delightfully normal. "Mommy! Luke! What are you doing here?"

Luke cut straight to the chase. "Sonya and Aiden have locked themselves in this closet. Can you get them to come out, please?"

"Well, yeah. Sure." She bounced across the room, tapped on the door twice, paused, then tapped twice again.

"Dorrie!"

"Dorrie, you're here!"

Two little voices chimed her name in unison.

Luke met the principal's curious glance. "That's the secret knock they use in their tree house at my place."

"Ah."

"Why are you guys in the closet?" Dorrie asked.

Not one of the adults had asked the kids why they'd locked themselves in there.

"Sonya was sad," Aiden explained.

Oh... Rainey's heart melted a little, thinking of how kind Luke's son must be.

"So she hid in the closet?" Dorrie's tone said that was kind of a dumb thing to do.

"No." Sonya's voice this time. "I went to a thinking place, like we do at Luke's. In the tree house. And Aiden said he wanted to think, too."

"Well, are you done?" Dorrie's voice hovered near impatience. "Because I've got things to do and if you're done thinking, then get out of there. Okay?"

"All right."

"Okay."

The adults waited, almost not breathing, watching for the handle to turn. Listening for the lock to disengage.

Click.

The tiny sound had them all breathing a sigh of relief. The door handle turned, paused, then turned again, and when the door swung outward, two little hands were clutching the knob.

"We did it!"

"Yeah, we did!" Aiden and Sonya high-fived each other, but their joyous expressions faded when they spotted the crowd of adults just outside the door.

Luke scooped up Aiden.

Rainey did the same to Sonya.

Dorrie arched a brow at both children. "Guys, you can't do that in kindergarten." She flounced her one tight ponytail for effect. "You have to stay in your chair and think."

Sonya rolled her eyes, amazed. "No one can do that."

Aiden sent Dorrie a similar look, then buried his head in Luke's shoulder.

"Let's walk down to my office, shall we?" Mr. O'Mara's request held a mixture of relief and consternation. "Miss Patterson, we'll let you return to the rest of your class."

Luke didn't seem relieved to have his kid out of a scrape as much as furious that this had happened in the first place.

Was there something wrong with Rainey that she wasn't so upset? She was amused, yes. Angry? Not so much.

But she and Miss Sonya would have a heart-to-heart talk about locking doors, once they got home.

Mr. O'Mara pointed to the bench outside his office. "If the kids would like to sit here while we talk, that would be fine."

"Fine?" Luke sputtered the word and held his son tighter. "Mr. O'Mara, nothing about this whole situation could be called *fine*. You put my kid at risk. You put Sonya at risk. I don't think it's a stretch to say that you put an entire kindergarten class at risk by not having a key to that art closet."

"Maybe not the whole kindergarten," Rainey murmured. When Luke stared at her, she shrugged.

"It's only big enough to hold two or three kids at a time, tops."

"This isn't funny." The clipped note in his voice underscored his emotion.

Rainey reached up to touch Aiden's cheek, then ruffled Sonya's hair. "It is, kind of. I think it shows great resourcefulness that these two took a calming technique you taught them and put it to good use. But next time, don't lock the door." She made eye contact with both kids, one at a time. "Locked doors are dangerous if we don't have a key."

"Exactly." Luke's glare said she'd finally made a good point.

"So we'll get a key for that door, but only grown-ups will use it. And if you need thinking time away from the other kids, what should you do?"

Sonya shrugged.

Aiden glared at her, much like his father was doing.

"Tell a grown-up," Rainey instructed. "Grown-ups are on your side. I promise." She settled a look of honest, trusting patience on each child in turn, praying the sincerity of her words would reach them. From what she could see, she was successful, and she wasn't afraid to thank God for that.

If only there was a similar way to comfort the distraught father standing opposite her. The deep contours of his face said calming him down wasn't going to be quite as easy.

* * *

Luke felt Aiden's body relaxing in his arms.

Mr. O'Mara looked more comfortable, too, as if he was buying Rainey McKinney's spiel.

Buying it? Of course he's buying it. She made perfect sense, while you were about to jump off the deep end, trying to make Aiden's life "Secret Service safe." Let the kid fly a little.

His mother had scolded him about that not long ago, and Luke didn't talk to her for nearly a week, but finally had to give in. First, because she was right. Second, because he couldn't go seven days without her chicken biscuit pie.

He drew a deep breath and felt his overanxious heart start to settle down.

"Mr. O'Mara, did you have something you wanted to add?" Seeming quite at ease, Rainey shifted her attention to the principal.

He shook his head. "I think you covered it all, Rainey."

"Then you—" Rainey set Sonya down and squatted next to her "—scoot back to your classroom, and behave yourself. The bus will bring you home in one hour."

"You're not taking me home now?" Sonya looked scared, as if worried what her teacher's reaction would be. Luke wondered the same thing himself, but Rainey simply shook her head.

"You need to be brave every day. And follow

directions. That's how life is, cupcake, and I'd be doing you no favor by babying you."

Luke wanted to hug Sonya. Reassure her. Tell her everything would be all right. Then hold her hand and take her home.

To his surprise, Sonya sent a resigned look to her mother, then walked slowly down the hall. She turned to glance over her shoulder as she stepped into the kindergarten room, but Rainey kept her gaze averted, as if she expected the daughter to follow directions.

And the kid did it.

Luke eyed Aiden.

He should do the same thing. Put his son down and let him go face the dragon lady on his own.

He started to set Aiden down, but the boy clung to his neck. He didn't say a word, didn't whimper or whine, but that stranglehold on Luke's neck spoke volumes. "I'm going to drop Aiden off with his sitter, then send him back on Monday."

"All right, Luke." Mr. O'Mara looked as if he wanted to say more, but thought better of it. The principal had made a wise choice, considering Luke's current mood.

He walked out of the building just behind Rainey and wasn't sure if she was hurrying to stay ahead of him, or to make certain she escaped before Sonya or Dorrie did something else. Either way, he needed to thank her. "Rainey."

She turned at the edge of the parking lot. "Yes?"

Luke shrugged his free shoulder. "Thank you. You stayed calm and levelheaded. It helped. A lot."

She waved him off as if it was nothing, but Luke knew better. Staying calm under pressure was a wonderful trait, something he prided himself on.

Except when it came to Aiden.

He followed her to her car at the back of the full lot. "Have you thought about what I said the other day?" He shifted the boy slightly in his arms. "You saw Dorrie in there. You heard how things went down. I think it could work in everyone's favor."

Rainey stood perfectly still for a long, drawn-out moment, then smiled at Aiden. "We've got nothing to lose, right?"

"Right."

She hesitated again, then nodded. "How about if I bring the girls over tomorrow afternoon? The store is busy on Saturday mornings, but if Noreen can take over by midday, we'd have a few hours together. Dorrie wants to show me the tree house and Sonya wants me to help her take care of the animals."

"Bring your barn boots," Luke warned. The image of Rainey hanging out in the barn, feeding his menagerie, brightened his thoughts. That was something he'd have to think about later.

Rainey laughed. "Will do. I'll see you tomorrow."

She slipped behind the wheel of her mother's car and backed out of the spot carefully. Aiden lifted his head and offered Luke a penitent expression. "I'm sorry." He whispered the words in a tragic voice, a voice that took Luke back nearly three years.

He hugged the little guy, withdrew the booster seat he kept in the cruiser's trunk, and fastened Aiden into the backseat. "No more locked doors, okay?"

Aiden nodded, but as Luke settled himself into the driver's seat, he glimpsed a tiny look of satisfaction on his son's face reflected in the rearview mirror. It vanished as soon as they made eye contact, but Luke hadn't gotten to be a decorated deputy by accident. The kid had smirked, knowing he'd pulled one over on his teacher, the principal and now his father.

Which meant Luke's mother was right. Again. Aiden knew how to play his dad and wasn't afraid to pull out all stops to avoid going to school. But what could Luke do about it other than order the kid to stay in class, in his seat, and pay attention?

Luke called his former sister-in-law and asked if she could watch Aiden an hour early. She agreed, and he headed to the opposite side of Kirkwood Lake, stewing over his choices.

Rainey's kid was back in class, following the rules.

His was heading home, essentially getting a reward for misbehaving.

Luke didn't have to wonder which kid learned the better lesson. The realization that Rainey had instinctively handled the situation more effectively than all the other adults around her, including him, made him realize he might have a thing or two to learn from Rainey McKinney himself.

Regret waged war with common sense as Rainey drove back to the farm. Sonya's expression of woe had tugged at Rainey's heart, even though she'd pretended ignorance.

"Better they cry now than you cry later...."

Her mother's words struck home. She'd gone easy on Rainey as a child. And Rainey had strayed from the right path and caused her mom grief. But they'd both learned a valuable lesson the hard way, and Sonya and Dorrie would benefit from it. She hoped.

Rainey's brain revved into overdrive as she passed the park sign: Kirkwood Lake Bicentennial Kickoff! Join us for a Fall Festival of fun and food as Kirkwood Lake begins its year-long, 200-years-young birthday celebration!

Piper and Lucia had reserved a festival spot during the bicentennial planning phases last spring. There was plenty of room to include a dairy booth. That would give Rainey a chance to meet folks, show them she'd changed and tempt them with the wonderful goods from the dairy store. Tackling the problem head-on might bring back old customers and attract new ones, crucial elements for the upcoming holiday season.

Can you do this? Face people, hour after hour, keeping your game face on?

Her resolve faltered as she turned into the farm driveway, but then she hauled in a deep, cleansing breath.

God had blessed her.

She was stronger now than she'd ever been. Sure, she'd take hits. After the cool welcome she'd encountered in town the first month, she'd be naive to expect otherwise.

But she was made of hardy stock, and endowed with a faith that moved mountains. Determined, she parked the car and dashed into the house for a notepad and pencil, before going on to the dairy store located behind the farmhouse. As she rushed through the empty dining room, the afternoon light shone on Christmas pictures of Dorrie and Sonya.

So much time gone. Memories Rainey could never be part of because she hadn't been here.

The twins were dressed alike in the first picture, but even then Dorrie's eyes had gleamed with mischief, while Sonya's gentle gaze begged for love. The next image showed them a year older, sitting with Santa at the Fireman's Hall. The girls had posed with the jolly old elf individually, then together in front of a huge Christmas tree. To the right of the tree was a beautiful crèche, carved figures of the Holy Family in a rugged wooden barn.

The final picture showed the girls last year, playing angels in a living Nativity scene sponsored by a local church. They'd been dressed in white bed-sheets, their latte-toned skin contrasting with their robes. Gold garland halos nestled against their dark hair. Beyond them lay a sheep and a lamb, while slightly older children played the parts of Mary, Joseph and the wise men.

It wrenched Rainey's heart.

She lifted the first picture, of the girls as adorable toddlers. Was she wrong to have left?

Probably. But her leaving had ensured the girls safety and that was what mattered. Rogue cops were nothing to be taken lightly, and bad cops who'd had witnesses disappear before?

They'd posed a direct threat thwarted by her whis-tle-blowing phone calls.

This year would be different. She wouldn't spend this Christmas alone, crying as she tended animals in an empty veterinary clinic outside Chicago. She'd be here in Kirkwood, with the girls and her mother. With Uncle Berto, Piper and the Harrison family next door. For the first time in three years Rainey wouldn't dread the change of seasons and the lonely holiday. This year she'd join in the celebration, be-cause this year she was home. And no matter what happened, she was home to stay.

She joined Noreen in the store and used the next few hours to roughly sketch how she'd like the dairy booth to look.

At seven o'clock, she closed the store and headed for the house, reenergized. The family gathered for a meeting each Friday night, where everyone aired ideas and compared notes. At tonight's get-together she'd convince them to let her put her best foot forward. No matter what, she had to make them listen to her concerns about the loss of business. And take action. Even if it meant Rainey had to find a different job. She crossed the wide yard and hurried into the house.

Wedding plans were spread out across the large dining room table. Farm notes were laid out in similar fashion in the kitchen.

"I saved food for you." Lucia smiled at Rainey as she came into the room. "Nice and warm, in the oven. You eat and we talk."

Food was the last thing on Rainey's mind, but her mom's caretaking was a welcome respite from the negativity she encountered whenever she stepped off the farm. "Thanks, Mama."

"Okay." Rainey's sister, Piper, called for attention as people grabbed seats. "Wedding first. Let's take thirty minutes to coordinate things and make sure we're synchronized."

"Are we planning a wedding or strategizing a battle plan?" Zach Harrison wondered, but then the New York State trooper flashed a smile toward his fiancée.

Piper leveled him a look, then laughed. "How can

we have seven adults in this family and not one of us has ever planned a wedding?"

Zach's father shrugged. "Zach's mother did all the work for Julia and Evan's wedding. My job was to sign the checks."

Zach held up ringless hands. "First-timer."

Piper acknowledged his hand and added, "And your only time, buster."

Her mom made a face of regret. So did Uncle Berto, Lucia's brother.

"Julia's planned a wedding. Maybe we should have her come over," Zach suggested. His sister was living in his house next door, until she closed on her own place two miles south.

Berto sprang out of his chair. "I will go watch her little boys and she can talk flowers and fancy cakes and things. On wedding day, I will be a bear." He drew up his shoulders to make himself look bigger. "Moving things, setting things up, taking things down, this I can do. Planning a party?" He strode to the door, looking relieved. "Miss Julia will be better equipped."

Lucia waved him on. "Go. It is a good idea. The boys like their uncle Berto."

"Me, too." Piper sent him a look of gratitude. "Thank you."

Julia joined them less than five minutes later. She carried a clipboard and had a pen stuck behind her ear. She walked in, scanned the planning notes on the table, and within thirty minutes had a timeline of the wedding day mapped out. "I'll transfer this to my laptop this weekend," she told them when they wrapped up the session. "And I'll email it to each of you. Notify me if anything changes and I'll keep it updated.

"Everything's been ordered," she continued. "We'll use the front barn for the reception if the weather turns bad, and we have six days after the wedding to get ready for the bicentennial festival. That takes us right into the holidays. We'll be fine as long as we pay attention to details."

Marty Harrison grinned at her. "You are your mother's daughter, for sure."

Julia's smile turned bittersweet. "I see Mom's face when I look in the mirror. But that could mean I'm getting old."

"That's my vote," Zach quipped.

Julia punched his arm, then laughed when he hugged her. "Mom would have loved seeing you get married." The wistful note in her voice said she missed their late mother. "And she'd adore Piper."

Zach nudged his future wife. "Me, too."

"And now, the farm plans." Piper moved to the kitchen table, but not before she met Zach's smile of appreciation with a wink. "The legal move to incorporate as Harrison-McKinney Farms will be completed next week." She high-fived Zach's father across the table. Their new partnership put McKinney Farms back on solid financial ground. Except for the current loss of business in the dairy store.

"But we'll keep the name McKinney Farms to avoid confusion," Marty added. "Keeping it simple is best for business and reputation."

"Marty's name will be added to the farm signs we've ordered, and it will be on our letterhead and all official documents."

"And Piper and I are going to the stock sale in early November to add a new line of heifers to our breed stock," Marty added. "By next fall we should have an overabundance of milk to supply the new Greek yogurt facility near I-90 and the dairy store."

"So all is good on that front." Piper turned toward Rainey. "And now the dairy store."

Rainey stood. She hated to be a downer at the family meeting, but the numbers gave her little choice. "We're losing money at the store and I believe it's because of me."

Lucia's lips thinned.

Piper's expression went from engaging to concerned in a flash. "Rainey, we always have a slowdown in September. Kids go back to school, ice cream sales drop. The days are getting shorter so people don't come out at night like they do over the summer. Then things pick up again in October and go crazy until the holidays."

Rainey acknowledged that with a nod as she passed a printed sheet to each of them. "That's all true, and it's supported by last year's figures, but here's the problem." She pointed out a group of highlighted numbers. "Our everyday stock items have dropped nearly twenty percent from last September's figures. That's huge. That eats up our profit margin and dumps us ten percent into the hole. And I think it's because some customers don't like who I was. That's a tough thing for folks to move past."

"We all make mistakes," Marty counseled. He shrugged lightly. "And people forget, Rainey. It just takes time."

"But can we survive for however long that takes?" Rainey wondered. "I know you want me to stay," she told everyone. "You're all being wonderful about this, but I have to do something to fix the situation or I'll go crazy worrying about it."

"Worry is not of God," Lucia reminded her. "He has taken care of us so far, *mi* Larraina. I trust He will take care of this, as well."

Rainey appreciated her mother's gesture of acceptance, but knew she needed to act quickly. "Well, I'd like to help the good Lord all I can, so here's what I'm proposing. We've got a farm booth signed up for the bicentennial festival. I'd like to have a dairy booth alongside. We've got portable coolers and the generator, we could use the space you've already reserved so we don't have to ask for extra space from the committee, and it would be a great way to give out samples of the new items we're going to carry for the holidays. I don't want Noreen outside all day if the weather during the festival is dicey, but Marly said she has no classes that Friday so she'll help me run the booth all day Friday and Saturday."

"You want to run the booth yourself?" Piper asked, glancing at her and Lucia with concern. "You're comfortable with that?"

What Piper meant was could she handle the knowing looks and possible nasty remarks people might make?

Rainey shrugged. "I love working in the dairy store and overseeing the milk production in the back room. And I like people. Right now, a lot of local folks don't trust me. Helping at the festival will give them a chance to see me in a new light. If we fix this now, it will have less impact on our holiday sales, and we all know that fourth-quarter sales could make or break the year for us."

"There could be repercussions," Zach cautioned. "Are you ready for that, Rainey? People might act stupid, given the chance."

"Yes." She answered with conviction, but fought the internal threat of foreboding. "Dad used to say 'Peace begins with a smile.'"

"Mother Teresa's saying." The reminder of their father's gentle ways made Piper smile.

"So." Zach brought them back to the practical. "What do we need for your booth? We'll make a list of supplies that Dad and I can get. You ladies have enough on your plates with the wedding. You tell me how you want the booth to look, and Dad and I will create it."

Rainey handed him a pencil sketch. "Done."

He laughed and pocketed the paper. "You don't waste time."

"Well, I used to." She sent the group a small grimace of remorse. "But not anymore. And the best steel comes from the toughest forging, right?"

"Amen."

The group started to disband, but Piper paused near Rainey before following Zach outside. "You've come a long way."

Rainey nodded.

"But I don't want you to push yourself too far. I want you to feel comfortable. At peace."

Rainey hugged her. "I will," she promised. "But I can't sit back and let things happen if there's a way to fix them. That's a quality I learned from you, Piper. And my mother."

"We'll do all we can," her sister promised.

"I don't move into my own house until the first week of November, and I'm not on call the weekend of the festival," Julia interjected. "Let me work the stand with you. It would give me a chance to meet people here. As long as Lucia would be willing to have the boys underfoot."

"Doing farm work won't bother you?" Rainey asked.

"Not at all. Why?"

"Well, you're a midwife now." Rainey reminded her, as if that was reason enough to bow out of festival farm help. "A professional."

Julia laughed. "Once a farm girl, always a farm girl. And while I wasn't big on the cows, I love the marketing stuff. Farm stands, fairs, the people. Sign me up, Rainey. I'm glad to help."

"Will do."

Rainey helped her mother straighten up the kitchen. Bags of freshly made croutons lined one counter, ready for sale. A list of chores sat alongside the bags. Lucia's organization and planning had helped make the farm business a slowly growing success over the past decade and a half. Now, with Marty's investment and partnership, McKinney Farms could become a flagship enterprise. This was the chance they'd all been waiting for.

"Rainey."

"Hmm?" She turned and was engulfed by her mother's warm embrace. She'd caused her mom so much grief over the years. She had no way to repay Lucia for her constant faith, which was so undeserved. Rainey hugged her mother back, but then

Lucia created a little distance between them and met her gaze.

"You are not to make yourself crazy over this." Lucia waved to the store. "We will do our best and people will come around, but I do not want you to back-step."

"Backslide." Rainey smiled at the misused word. "I won't, Mama, I—"

"I say this because I know my daughter best," Lucia insisted. "I knew you were not guilty of that crime and I know you wear this too much on your heart. I don't want for you to have more nightmares. More pain."

Nightmares had dogged Rainey after her prison stint, but she was better these days. Most of the time. "I'm stronger now. Don't worry. Didn't you just tell me worry is not what God wants for us?"

Lucia sighed and frowned. "Yes, but—"

"No buts. I'm taking the girls over to Luke Campbell's house tomorrow afternoon once the store quiets down. If Marly and Noreen need help, can they call you?"

"Of course. But Luke Campbell? How did you meet him?"

"At the school," Rainey explained. "It seems our children enjoy being naughty together."

Lucia's broad face split into a smile. "That is quite true. Each one thinking of some new way to put gray in my hair, but so sweet. Sweeter, though, when they sleep."

Rainey laughed. "Well, we're trying to work together to make them more comfortable in school. And maybe I can get the twins to help with the festival project."

"And being with the girls is good for his boy." Lucia nodded, satisfied. "I think this is good. His family is big and nice and they care for each other always."

Her words reminded Rainey of the family she'd longed for as a child. She'd wanted the American dream. *The Cosby Show* come to life. Even after her mother married Tucker McKinney, money problems were pervasive. Getting the farm back on solid ground after Tucker's wife had taken her share of the farm's assets had been a struggle of work, work and more work.

Rainey had rebelled, too immature to realize that God blessed the work of human hands.

She'd been a foolish child, then a disrespectful teenager, but she'd changed. Now if she could only convince the community of that.

Chapter Three

On Saturday afternoon Luke scrubbed damp palms against the sides of his jeans and frowned.

Why did Rainey's impending arrival with the twins make him nervous? Piper had brought the girls over plenty of times in the past.

This isn't Piper.

This was Rainey, the bad-girl sister, the object of community-wide speculation, most of it negative.

He firmed his jaw, determined to keep things easy, friendly, and then she pulled into the driveway. The girls tumbled out of the backseat, laughing and racing to join Aiden in the tree house, with barely a hello to Luke.

He scarcely saw them. His attention was drawn to Rainey. His breath caught somewhere deep in his chest as she stepped out of the car. She'd clipped her long wave of hair into some kind of barrette behind her head. The hairstyle accented the perfect oval of her face, the high cheekbones, the delicate arch of her neck and throat. A tiny gold cross hung on a thin chain. She watched the girls race across the yard, then turned his way.

She saw his expression. Read his look.

She stood perfectly still, her eyes on his, and for the life of him, Luke didn't want to break the connection. Finally, he moved forward, feeling like a gawky teen. "Hey."

"Hey." She flashed him a quiet smile and arched one brow in the direction of the tree. "They're fine up there?"

"Have been so far. Notice I put rails around the edge, so they can't fall."

"Except from the ladder."

He nodded. "I was thinking of adding a cushioned landing for them, just in case."

"Or don't, so they learn to hold on tight, because it really isn't all that high."

Luke sucked in a breath. Her advice sounded like something his family would say. "Life comes with enough peril attached."

Rainey moved toward the tree house as she answered. "The more prepared we are, the better our chances of survival."

"You think I baby Aiden."

She turned, still smiling, and he saw no censure in her gaze. "I don't know you well enough to make an assumption like that, and I'm stumbling through parenthood myself, so I'm not about to judge you on your methods." Her tone didn't condemn, it offered acceptance, and that felt good to Luke after the verbal scoldings he'd been getting lately. "I know life is a precious gift, and God expects us to take care of our children, heart and soul. That's a balancing act right there."

"Mommy, see?" Dorrie peered over the railing and waved to them. "Isn't this the best tree house ever?"

"Amazing." She drew the word out to underscore her approval, which shone in her face. Her eyes. The autumn sun silhouetted her profile, and Luke thought he'd never seen a more beautiful sight.

"Mommy! Come see!" Sonya joined Dorrie at the tiny "porch" of the tree house. "You'll love it up here!"

"Here I come." She scrambled up the short ladder and faked a gasp. "Is that your kitchen?"

Aiden laughed out loud, a sound Luke didn't hear often enough. "Yes. Daddy made it."

She looked down at Luke, and he had to act fast to pretend he wasn't appreciating the sight of her in her jeans. He wasn't quite speedy enough, however, and the look she sent him—half scolding, half amused—said she didn't really mind his admiration. She ignored the moment and indicated the interior of the tree house. "How'd you get that little kitchen set in there?"

"Classified information, ma'am."

She studied him, then the tree house while the children giggled, buzzing like happy little bees at a hive. "You built it around the kitchen set?"

"Nope."

She frowned, tapping her chin with one tawny-skinned finger, while the kids waited for her next guess. "The shoemaker's elves put it together at night?"

"I only wish that was true."

Sonya clapped a hand over her mouth, as if eager to spill the beans. Dorrie pretended to be calm. Aiden jumped up and down in tiny hops, excited to see what came next, and that made Luke's smile widen. His son didn't take to folks quickly, and that was partially Luke's fault for sheltering him.

"Aha." She aimed a triumphant look at the little ones, then him. "You took it in there piece by piece and assembled it inside."

"Yes!" Aiden pumped his fist in the air. "How did you guess that?"

"Isn't it wonderful, Mommy?"

"Don't you just love it?"

She laughed, handed out kisses to the excited children, then climbed back down. Luke offered his hand when she was on the last rung of the ladder, and she hopped off, her eyes shining up at him and the three kids. "I'd have picnics in there all the time if I had a tree house like this."

"Can we have one today, Luke?"

"Please?"

"Please, Daddy?"

Luke made a show of eyeing his watch. "It's past lunch and not nearly suppertime."

"Perfect for high tea, then," Rainey announced.

"High what?" Luke made a face at her, and the kids giggled above.

"Also known as snack time. But for the royals among us—" Rainey did a deep bow, with a hand flourish in the direction of the children "—it's referred to as high tea. Have you such makings in your house, old chap?"

Luke rolled his eyes and the kids giggled harder. "Let us go hence into the house and see, m'lady."

"Young royals, we shall return with haste to grace your table with the finest of foods and drink." She bowed again and headed toward the house with Luke. "Aren't you worried they might fall while we're gone?" she whispered.

"I worry about everything," he confessed, and the simple admission made him worry less. "It's ridiculous."

"Not when it all lands on your shoulders," she told him as he swung open the wooden screen door. "Oh, Luke. This house." She paused on the steps and drank in the pretty porch. "This is utterly beautiful."

"Thank you."

"What a marvelous place to grow up." She looked

out to the barns, the sheds, the well-treed lot and the gravel drive. "It's the picture of country living. And you must have a ball decorating this porch for Christmas with garlands and twinkle lights. Have you owned it a long time?"

Garlands? Twinkle lights? Guilt found new lodging in his chest as he thought of the artificial tree he stuck in the living room corner every year, using two strings of lights and two dozen satin balls from Walmart. "Nearly three years."

"Well, it's meant to inspire roots."

"Now if I could only figure out the whole 'wings' part of the equation that every child psychologist talks about," he remarked as he led her into the kitchen. "Encouraging Aiden to take a chance is the tough part for me."

"He's five, he's cute and he's getting spunkier. He just needs to spread those wings on his own a little. Take a few falls." She nodded toward the tree house, visible through the wide picture window above the sink. "And I can see I'm not telling you anything you don't already know," she added, "so let me just say this kitchen is absolutely lovely. And clean. Which is kind of scary, for a single dad."

"He has help," a woman's voice interjected.

Rainey turned, surprised. So did Luke.

"Hillary. I wasn't expecting you to stop by." Luke offered his former sister-in-law a puzzled look.

"Sorry, I came through the back door to grab my

file bag from yesterday." The woman lifted a black canvas tote in her left hand. "I wanted to copy some notes into my laptop and realized they were still here. Oops."

It didn't take a college degree to read the other woman's ruse, which meant maybe Rainey shouldn't be here. But Luke seemed to think nothing of the explanation. Of course, he was a man and more than likely oblivious.

"I'm Hillary Baxter, Luke's sister-in-law. I help him with Aiden." Cool and crisp, Hillary nodded toward the tree house outside the back door. "You're the twins' mother."

"Rainey McKinney. Nice to meet you."

Hillary offered a thin smile. "Yes, well. I have to go. Duty calls."

Luke set down a box of crackers he'd pulled from the cupboard and nodded. "I'll see you Monday."

"I'll *be* here."

Her tone hinted she belonged here, Rainey didn't. Hillary exited through the back door and made a show of climbing the ladder, clutching Aiden in a huge hug, reminding him twice to stay away from the opening, and then hugging him again, whispering something.

Rainey fought the urge to choke. The other woman was pretty and accomplished. Her style and grace shone like well-rinsed fresh pearls. Perfect hair, great shoes, tailored pants and a silk shirt.

Who wore silk to visit a kid?

Luke handed over a jar of peanut butter. "Can you spread this on those crackers? And I have some little fancy cupcakes from the store. I think they'd be high-tea stuff, right?"

"Perfect."

"We don't have to make tea, do we?"

"Not this time," she told him. "Juice boxes will do the trick. And please note that the children are playing nicely, they've scrambled up and down that ladder at least a dozen times to gather treasures from under the trees, and no one has fallen."

"Yet."

"Oh, ye of little faith," she chided him. She gave him a tiny elbow thrust to drive home her words. "Our instincts for survival tell us to hang on. To watch our step."

"Preach that to me after your first trip to the E.R. on a busy Saturday."

She nodded. "Good point. I might be singing a different tune then. Okay, peanut butter crackers, tiny cupcakes with sprinkles, and juice boxes. Our high tea is ready."

She'd fussed about, putting everything on a foil-covered cookie sheet because he didn't own a fancy tray. He thought the whole thing silly until he saw the kids' eyes go wide as Rainey and he approached.

"This is so fancy!"

"Oh, I love it, Mommy!"

"Daddy, this is a great party!"

Luke's heart swelled as he climbed the ladder. Rainey lifted the tray up to him, and as it changed hands, their gazes met again.

Sheer beauty.

And it wasn't because of her lovely face, her gold-toned skin or the soft tumble of hair.

It was her spirit, shining through the smile she gave him.

His chest tightened, as it did the week before when he'd first laid eyes on her. But inside, his heart melted.

Think, man. She's got a troubled history. And even if she didn't commit the crime she did time for, she was part of the gang that held up that store.

He knew all that. Rainey's teenage years had been nothing but trouble, but in all his years on the force, he'd seen a lot of kids change their lives. Why not her? Why not now?

You're willing to risk Aiden's well-being? You're a grown man. He's a kid who's already drawn the short straw on mothers once. Leave it alone.

Luke had to. He knew it.

But ignoring this attraction to Rainey was the last thing he wanted to do.

She curtsied to the trio in the tree. "And when you're finished with that, young royals, I'll be sure to tidy up the castle forthwith."

Her poor imitation of a highbrow British accent made them giggle. They ducked inside the little house, and their delighted voices made Luke silence the voices nagging him. "This was a great idea."

Rainey aimed a wistful look at the tree house. "I missed a lot of tea parties while I was gone. I need to make that up to them."

He longed to offer words of comfort, but they'd be just that. Empty words.

She noted his silence with a resigned look. "But I'm back now and determined to be a good mother."

He couldn't address that subject honestly, so he opted for a new topic, a safe one and hoped she didn't notice his lack of segue. "How are the wedding plans coming? Everything going all right?"

His quick change of subject said Luke found her former actions reprehensible. Well, so did she, but that was then. This was now. "Quite well. We had a family meeting last night and all systems are go."

He laughed. "My mother helped with my brothers' weddings. She was insanely busy during the planning. And there wasn't much I could do to help except haul furniture around. And deliver stuff."

After seeing her uncle's reaction the night before, Rainey completely understood. "Uncle Berto said the same thing. Still, those are important tasks when you've got a big party planned. And we're adding a dairy section to our farm booth for the festival the week after, so I've got to make sure I have everything set for that. The wedding, the booth, the store, decorating."

"That's an ambitious project," he mused. "Do you need a generator? I've got a portable one. I'm doing a petting zoo with the crew—" he motioned toward the barn "—but I don't need electricity. They'll have the park lights on, and temporary lights will be strung around the perimeters."

"I could use an extra generator as backup. I don't want anything to go wrong."

He crossed the yard and sat down at the round picnic table under a sprawling maple tree. "Who's manning the booth?"

"Me."

His hesitation said he wasn't oblivious to the talk around town.

"Julia and Marly are helping." Rainey met his gaze frankly. "I think it's best for people to see me. Talk to me. It's time for folks to accept me as the adult I am, not the brat I was."

"You think it's that easy?" Luke's face mirrored the concern in his voice, and it wasn't hard to see the born protector in the man sitting opposite her.

"On the contrary, I think it will be very difficult. But sales are down since I took over the dairy store, and I can't take the chance that my presence is hurting the farm. So I'll do whatever it takes to make sure that doesn't happen."

Luke whistled softly. "That's a lot to take on your shoulders, Rain."

Her heart sighed.

The way he shortened her name sounded just right, coming from him. Sweet. Personal.

But there were multiple reasons why they could never be sweet and personal, so she ignored the adrenaline rush and redirected her attention to the far barn. "Can we meet the horses?"

"Aiden and Sonya will insist on introducing you to the entire menagerie, so yes. Absolutely. We can head over there now. The kids will find us."

"Make them clean up the tree house first," she instructed him. "You don't want mice and rats up there, feasting after the kids are done."

"The cats help keep them at bay."

She nodded. "They do at the farm as well, but there's no use tempting them into a kids' play area, right? Do you have a whisk broom?"

"No. Nor do I even know what a whisk broom is. And don't tell me you have one in your mother's trunk, because that's way too Mary Poppins."

"Mary Poppins is preferable to my current image in town," she told him. "Maybe you've got a short-handled broom in the barn?"

"I do."

"Perfect."

They approached the far paddock, and Rainey didn't hesitate to climb the rungs of fencing, tempting the horses her way. The two mares shifted her a look, touched noses and proceeded to ignore her, kind of like the reaction she got from the kindergarten teachers, but the aged gelding walked her way, sensing a friend.

"Yes, old boy, hello." She crooned the words and looped an arm around the horse's neck. "Aren't you just a love? And so beautiful, such a pretty shade of chestnut. What's your name?"

"Spirit."

She turned to Luke and smiled as the horse rubbed his cheek along her shoulder, begging to be stroked. "What a perfect name."

"He was part of the county's mounted patrol for over a decade. A few years after Spirit retired, the fellow that owned him died. His son took over the place and Spirit fell on hard times for half a dozen years."

"Abused."

"And neglected, underfed, unshod, long-in-the-tooth." Luke reached over her head to scratch the old horse's head. "I found him on a rescue call and brought him here."

"Well, he's gorgeous." She touched her forehead against the horse's neck, the scents of farm, barn, hay and horse a welcome home she'd missed. "I never realized how lucky I was to grow up on a farm until I was out in the big world and saw what the general population has to do to survive. Kids are so oblivious to the beauty that surrounds them. I was, anyway."

"I think most of us are. Except our current quiet moment is about to be shattered."

"Mommy, you're meeting the horses!" Sonya raced to Rainey's side and reached out to pet Spirit's flank. "Hey, Spirit, this is my mommy. And that's Bella over there." She pointed across the paddock. "And that's Oh My Stars, but we just call her Star."

"They're beautiful, Sonya."

"Can we go around back to see the other animals?" Dorrie begged.

"Dad, let's show her the goats. And the sheep."

"And baby lambs," Dorrie offered in a singsong voice, much as Rainey had done to the old horse.

Rainey turned to hop off the rail, but paused when Luke grasped her waist to help her down.

Firm. Strong. Rugged. Gentle.

All those qualities came through that simple touch, his hands gripping her middle as he set her onto firm ground.

She couldn't look up, not just yet. He'd see the effect he had on her, and neither one of them could afford to cross the line they'd drawn in the sand.

He didn't wait for her to look up. He ducked his

head to see her and shoved his hands pointedly into his pockets. "We're in trouble, Rain."

She knew exactly what he meant, but shook her head firmly. "No, we're not. We won't allow ourselves to be."

His bemused grin said they'd passed that point somewhere back in that school parking lot, and she worried the inside of her cheek, knowing he was right, but determined to prove him wrong. As long as he kept his hands, looks and smiles to himself.

Their eyes met as they rounded the corner, and his expression said he understood.

But then he smiled, which indicated he kind of liked their current roller coaster of emotions, and if she was totally honest with herself, she did, too. Which was another reason to make sure she applied the brakes, ASAP.

Dorrie skipped ahead, leading the way into the second barn. Then she sighed, exasperated, and led them back out the other side. "I forgot, Luke."

"And then you remembered."

She nodded and dashed around the perimeter fencing. "Luke says that animals like being outside on nice days, just like kids. So they'll be over here, not in the barn."

"I want to show her the sheep!"

"They're my sheep. I get to show her!"

"Aiden, that's selfish!"

"Mom!"

"Dad!"

Rainey stooped to their level as they curved around the rustic fencing. "How about you all show me? Dorrie, you tell me the ewe's name. And Aiden, you and Sonya introduce me to the lambs."

"But there are three babies." Aiden's frown said that didn't add up, but then he grinned and pointed to his father. "Dad can tell you the last baby's name."

"That's fair," Luke supposed. As they approached the sheep pen, the sight of three little lambs, cozied together in the shade of a small wooden hutch, made Rainey sigh again. Their white fleece gleamed against golden wheat straw, and the image was like a shot from an old-world Nativity scene. "Oh, how precious! Aren't they the sweetest things?"

Luke met her eyes, his expression saying the lambs might have some stiff competition today.

That look made Rainey long to be the sweetest thing in Luke Campbell's life.

She was anything but that, so she turned back to the animals.

"They're using these guys for the living Nativity at my parents' church this year." Arms loose on the uppermost rail, Luke turned his attention back to the lambs. "Testy O'Brien is bringing a somewhat stubborn donkey, and in lieu of camels, my three alpacas will take the place of the wise men's mounts."

A living Nativity scene. Home for the holidays. Christmas with her girls.

Tough emotions rose within Rainey. For the past three years, she'd volunteered to oversee the vet clinic and kennel in Oak Park, allowing others to spend the day with family, hoping to feel less alone.

She'd wept as she cared for the small creatures, wishing things were different. Wishing *she* was different.

But now she was back home, with her girls and her family. And a chance to have a real Christmas together.

She swallowed hard, pushing rough emotions aside as she grasped hold of the here and now. "That will be beautiful, Luke."

He made a face. "My mother's idea, and I've got the animals, so why not let her have her fun?"

"Grandma said I could help," Aiden added. "But I have to dress warm."

"Can we help, Mommy? Like we did last year?"

"Yes, can we?"

"We'll see." She didn't dare make promises she might not be able to keep. But if she could, she'd have the girls at that living Nativity, marveling at the simplicity of Christ's birth.

Chapter Four

Bubble-bath clean, his short curls still damp, Aiden dived into bed, and Luke breathed in his scent. The boy's innocence took him back to those first years, holding his baby son, so perfect, so awesome. They should have been the quintessential family, Mom, Dad, beautiful baby boy.

What wretchedness had stolen Martha's self-confidence, or had Luke been fooling himself all along?

Maybe both, he realized as he read *Where the Wild Things Are* for the tenth time in as many days. And then he did a mine sweep underneath the bed to assure his son that none of Max's yellow-eyed friends lingered in Aiden's room.

Luke kissed him good-night, straightened the covers, then paused when Aiden said, "I think this was the very best day of my life, ever! Thanks, Dad."

"You're welcome."

He didn't have to dissect the boy's emotions to

figure out his meaning. The girls had been regular visitors over the past two years. And he'd gone to the McKinneys' farm just as often.

The difference today was Rainey. Her warmth, her attitude, her calm acceptance. Her presence turned snack time into a royal event. Her composure helped the kids think anything was possible.

Aiden hadn't wanted the day to end.

Neither had Luke.

The boy had begged for the girls to stay for supper.

Rainey declined gently, then explained there would be other days to get together soon. And that if Aiden followed directions, she and Luke would make sure it happened often.

Aiden believed her, and that in itself was a step forward. And now he was falling asleep, a happy child, a mood his father longed to sustain.

Sleep was the last thing on Luke's mind, but his grown-up dreams weren't made of make-believe. A lawman and father had to see the big picture. Yes, she was beautiful, and no male on the planet could ignore that.

But it wasn't the superficial that drew him, it was the wounded spirit within her, and that's what he needed to avoid. Pained souls called to him, like the menagerie of livestock living in his barns.

His phone rang. He glanced at the readout, saw

his mother's number and clicked on it. "Hey, Mom. What's up?"

"Dad's taking the boat out tomorrow. The weather's supposed to be wonderful. He wanted to know if you and Aiden would like to hang out over here."

"We'd love it." Luke sank into a wide-backed chair. "What time is good?"

"We're going to church first, so anytime after eleven."

"That will give me plenty of time to take care of the animals," Luke noted. He ignored the church reference. His mother left it alone as well, and that was almost worse than her nagging him.

Jenny Campbell didn't hassle. She dropped little pearls of wisdom into innocent conversation and then let her children wallow in free will. But she and Dad were always there to pick up the pieces as needed.

That brought Luke back to the whole roots-and-wings thing. "Can I bring company?"

"Of course. Who?"

"Rainey McKinney and I are trying to train our naughty children into better behavior by working together with them. If she and the twins are available, I'd like to bring them along."

"I'll throw another chicken in the pot."

Her comment made him laugh. There was always too much food at the Campbell house on weekends, but nothing ever went to waste. A phone call here or there brought folks over for an impromptu feast, and his mother's calm but active nature kept it all running like a well-oiled machine. "See you tomorrow."

Should he call Rainey now? He glanced at the clock, realized it wasn't too late and dialed the farm.

"McKinney Farms, Piper speaking."

"Piper, it's Luke. Is Rainey around?"

She coughed once, a short, odd-sounding cough, then cleared her throat. "Right here, actually. Hang on."

"Luke?"

"Hey." He paused to breathe, savoring the way the single syllable of his name rolled off Rainey's tongue. "My mom just called and invited us out on the lake tomorrow. I was wondering if you and the girls would like to go."

"Oh, I'd love it." There was no mistaking the upbeat note in her voice, and that made Luke smile. "But I can't. I'm working all day tomorrow. After church, that is."

"Well…" He thought for a few seconds, then asked, "How about if I take the girls? Dad and I will be in the boat with them, and we've got plenty of safety vests. Would that be okay?" When she hesitated, he added, "We did promise that if they were good, we'd get them together again soon. I do believe those were your exact words."

"They were. Little did I know I'd rue them so quickly, but you're correct. The girls gave me no trouble about coming home, grabbing a sandwich, getting showered and tucked into bed."

"So let's reward them as promised. And my mother always has plenty of food."

"Then yes, they can go, Luke." Rainey's voice assumed a more definite tone. "You're right, we want to reward good behavior quickly so they get the point. But can you have them back here by six for supper? That way I can get them settled and into bed by eight."

"Sure."

"And how about if you and Aiden have supper with us?"

His pulse thrummed.

Taking the girls out on the boat was a friendly thing. Having supper at the farm with Rainey and the twins?

Luke bit back what he knew he should say and nodded, unseen. "I'd like that."

"Me, too."

Two words, almost whispered. Two little words that shouldn't touch his heart, but did.

She was off-limits for more reasons than he could count, but when he was with her, none of that mattered.

"See you tomorrow. I'll be by around noon to pick up the girls."

"Okay."

He hung up the phone and stared at it, half torn, half pleased.

He probably shouldn't be seeing Rainey again this soon. He suspected she knew it, as well. But he was seeing her, and right or wrong, that made him happy. For today, that was enough.

A cool, well-dressed blonde with great hair moved across the aisle when Rainey and the girls slipped into a pew at church the next morning.

The gray-haired woman behind Rainey sniffed, clearly unhappy.

And several folks seated closer to the front swept her a glance as they turned, pretending they were looking at something or for someone, but then their eyes strayed to Rainey, as if challenging her reason to be there.

"Rainey! Good morning!" Pastor Smith's wife bustled down the aisle and reached out to give her a quick and conspicuous hug. "So nice to have you back. And these two, I just love them!" She directed a look of pleasure at the twins. "They're a handful at this age, but there's not a day goes by that I don't miss it, Rainey. Drink up this time with them."

"I will."

Piper slid in with Zach from the left, taking the seat the blonde had vacated. Rainey's mother and uncle stepped in from the right. Marty took a seat directly behind them. The older woman seated next to him stopped her huffing, surrounded by McKinneys.

Yet when Rainey was on her own, it was okay to act insulting.

She stood up straight, shushed the girls gently and opened her hymnal as the opening notes of the piano sounded through the sanctuary, a song of peace, hope and love.

She longed for all three, but what were the chances when her very presence upset so many?

Rainey stood with her family, flanked by good people, people who trusted her heart. But did she have the right to put them at financial risk because she wanted to regain her standing in the family?

They would shrug off the peril.

She couldn't. And that meant she had to make sure the dairy store stayed successful, or find another job.

There was always work in Clearwater, the small city at the lake's southern tip, even if it wasn't high-paying. If that was the trade-off she needed to make, she'd do it, because end-of-year sales were huge in the area. Some folks would head south for the winter. Others wouldn't travel around the lake to buy fresh milk, bread and eggs in the snow. She wanted to head into the holidays with strong sales and happy customers.

But right now, with the family surrounded by

negativity in the sweet, small church? Her goal seemed pretty impossible.

Luke pulled into the McKinneys' driveway, rolled to a stop and wasn't surprised when Aiden beat him out of the car.

The twins banged through the wooden screen door, one after the other. "Aiden, we're going out on the boat!" Dorrie screeched.

"May I sit with you on the boat, Luke?" Sonya asked in a much softer tone.

"Sure can." He ruffled her hair. "And my dad's going to be with us, too, so we can go exploring."

"I love going out on the water," Dorrie announced as she marched to the car. "Bye, 'Buela! Love you!"

Lucia waved in response as she approached Luke. "One is eager, one is cautious."

He swept Aiden and Sonya a quick glance. "Which is why we're trying to push from different directions. Hoping for a more even keel."

"I think this can work," Lucia agreed, then noted his eyes straying to the door. "Rainey is working at the store, if you wish to say goodbye."

He wanted to but wouldn't.

Friends. She'd made the pronouncement; he'd agreed. To push for more would be wrong. Except it felt too right to be wrong, but he didn't have time to explore that now, and he wasn't exactly an expert when it came to relationships.

He shook his head and herded the kids to the car. "We're good. Rainey knows I'm taking them, and the afternoons are getting short. I'll have them back by six, like I promised."

Lucia hugged each kid in turn, then waved them off. "Have fun! *Vaya con Dios, mi bebés preciosas!*"

"See you later!"

"Bye!"

Luke eased the car around the circular drive. It took all his energy not to pause and dash into the dairy store, but he made it, and then regretted his fortitude all the way to his parents' place on the east shore.

But once they pulled into the Campbell complex overlooking the lake's point, his thoughts were taken over by a small woman affectionately labeled "Hurricane Jenny."

"Girls, hello!" His mother burst through the side door, ready to hug anything she could catch. "Aiden! Sonya! Dorrie! How are you guys? Ready for a boat trip with Grandpa?"

"I am." Dorrie nodded, hugged Luke's mother and then raced to where his father was readying the boat at the end of the dock. "Grandpa Charlie, how are you?"

"Me, too." Aiden smiled up at his grandmother and arched a brow. "But Dad said you might have cookies here if we were good."

"Always, Aiden. You know that. Go see Grandpa,

I think he's ready for you." She turned and bent to Sonya's level. "Nice to see you again, sweetie."

Sonya smiled and twisted a lock of hair with one finger. "Luke said I could sit with him."

"Well, what girl can resist that?" his mother quipped. She gave Sonya a quick hug before sending her toward the boat. "Have fun. I'll have cookies and milk waiting when you get back from your adventure."

The five-year-old turned. "This is an adventure?"

His mother nodded. "Absolutely."

Sonya's eyes widened. "My mom says it's good to have adventures. And to be big and brave and bold all the time."

"Your mother is smart," Jenny replied. "Moms always want their kids to be big and brave and bold." Was it a coincidence that she angled a look Luke's way at that moment?

Nope. Jenny didn't do coincidences. She was tight with God and a longtime mother, so making a point without a lecture was a practiced skill. Luke gave her a hug before following the kids to the boat. "See you in a little while."

"There'll be family here when you get back."

"Always is."

Family was a given on Sundays. Everyone was welcome. But he'd be busy with three kids, so he might have to miss Seth's football laments and Jack's lectures on getting a life. Max was stationed at Fort Bragg for at least another year and Cassidy was working in Buffalo. Addie had just gotten a job as an instructor at St. Bonaventure College and Marcus was finishing a two-year clerking stint for a federal judge in D.C.

They might seem far-flung, but they were Campbells at heart, all for one and one for all. Family gatherings strained the walls of his parents' sprawling home now that grandchildren entered the picture. And Luke wouldn't have it any other way.

"I'm making myself scarce," Piper announced as she came downstairs late Sunday afternoon. "We're having dinner at Zach's place. I'd have you come along, but you've got supper well in hand, Rainey."

"Just simple stuff," she replied, but didn't miss the look her sister sent her way. "They're bound to be hungry, don't you think?"

"Luke's mother is an amazing cook, so I wouldn't bet on it, but I'm impressed that you went to all this trouble to feed the girls when a peanut butter sandwich would do."

Rainey's nonchalant shrug made Piper laugh. "Did you think I wouldn't notice you cooked enough for an army? You think he'll stay?"

"He's welcome to," was all Rainey would say. "Aiden needs more time out and about. Away from—" She bit her tongue and said no more.

"Hillary?"

"You know her?" Rainey turned, glanced at the clock and saw they had a few more minutes. "She's a little overbearing."

Piper made a face. "Your description is more than kind, and I've been telling Luke for over a year that she babies Aiden too much, but he feels bad because his wife was Hillary's fraternal twin. Losing Martha was hard on her."

"Losing a young mother is hard on everyone," Rainey remarked. "It's never easy to say goodbye. Was she sick for a long time?"

Piper's expression went quiet, but then the crunch of wheels on gravel pushed her to the door. "Lucia and Berto are eating with us. You've got the house to yourself."

Matchmaking.

That's why her mother and uncle had hightailed it out half an hour ago. And Piper ducked out the front door as Luke and the kids burst through the kitchen entrance.

"Mommy, Grandpa Charlie made the boat go in circles!"

"And he went superfast over some waves and we almost tipped over!"

"And then he showed us where the swans live, but he said they're going to go far away for the winter and they'll come back when it's warm again, but I don't get that because it's warm here." Dorrie splayed her hands, indicating her shorts and T-shirt.

"So why don't they just stay? Because I like them. They're very pretty."

"They remind me of fairy tales," Sonya whispered. She hugged Luke's leg. "Thank you for taking us to see them, Luke."

He swooped her up and returned the hug. "You're welcome, toots. I'm glad you had fun. Grandpa Charlie had fun, too. And today's weather was the exception, not the rule, Dorrie." He grinned down at her as he palmed her head. "I expect by the time you unpack those shorts next spring, you'll have outgrown them."

"Too true. How about you, Aiden?" Rainey squatted to his level. "Which did you like best? Going fast, spinning in circles or seeing the swans?"

"I just like being with my daddy." He tipped a sweet smile up to Luke, and Rainey saw the big guy melt on the spot.

"Well, I like being with your daddy, too," Dorrie announced, "but I mostly liked spinning!" She whirled dizzily, laughing as she tumbled onto the couch.

"I can spin, too!" Aiden darted into the living room and mimicked her, giggling all the while.

"Watch out for the kittens," Rainey warned. "They're loose out there."

"Kittens!"

"Sweet!"

Three little bodies scrambled to the floor, peering

beneath upholstery skirting, hunting up tiny four-legged friends.

"Something smells amazing." Luke walked to the stove, lifted a lid and turned Rainey's way. "Did you make pulled pork?"

She nodded. "And yellow rice and corn. Are you hungry?"

"Starved," Dorrie announced as she came to the table. "Grandma Jenny had chicken and biscuits at their house and I ate some. Sonya said no, thank you, and Aiden just wanted cookies."

"Ah. Well…" Rainey lifted the lid on a rectangular pan. "I made a milk cake for dessert, but you have to eat some supper first."

"A milk cake?" The word *cake* grabbed Aiden's interest. He moved closer. "Do you eat it with milk? Because I like milk and cake."

"You made *tres leches* cake?" Luke peeked over her shoulder and his sigh tickled the soft skin just below her ear. "From scratch?"

"There is no other proper way to make milk cake," she scolded. "There is the right way and there is the wrong way. This is the right way."

"You like to cook."

He was close. Too close. And yet not close enough, so she slipped from beneath his arm and moved a few feet away as she retrieved dishes from the cupboard. "I like to create. Cooking for cooking's sake isn't much fun, but a clean kitchen makes me want to jump in and make something. Your kitchen is amazing, by the way."

"Because it gets little use," he admitted. "I grill on the nights I'm home. Even in winter. Or throw stuff in the oven. And the microwave is an amazing invention."

Rainey thought of her time away. Tuna, ramen noodles and mac and cheese had been her mainstays. She'd felt like the true prodigal coming home to a full pantry, a larder of food, homegrown meats and vegetables fresh-frozen for use year-round. She hadn't realized the wonder of her mother until she was away from the goodness of a stocked kitchen. She grew up fast and hard while working on her own in Illinois, but she had grown up, finally.

Luke took the plates out of her hands. "You cooked. I'll set the table. Where's the silverware?"

"Here. But Dorrie and Sonya and Aiden can do that."

Dorrie dashed over. "I claim the spoons."

Sonya followed more quietly. "I'll do the forks."

"Aiden?" Rainey held out five butter knives. "Can you put the knives around the table, please? Put one next to each plate?"

"We're eating at the table?" Eyes wide, he accepted the knives and followed Dorrie and Sonya, setting one at each place. "I love eating at the table!"

Luke made a poor attempt to hide his guilty expression. Rainey made a guess as she withdrew three small jelly jars for glasses. "Tray tables in front of the TV?"

His silence said she'd nailed it.

"Good to see you realize your mistake, Deputy." She handed each child a glass and Luke raised a hand.

"You're letting them use real glass?"

"Of course. It's fancier that way."

"We love eating fancy," Dorrie assured him.

Sonya gave a quick nod. "Mommy says if we take care of nice things, we can have more nice things someday." She held up the eight-ounce jelly jar and her look of appreciation made Luke smile. "I want fancy glasses like this when I grow up."

"Me, too," sighed Dorrie.

The girls' wishes inspired Luke, while Rainey's wisdom hit home. Through a series of little things, she was raising her daughters' awareness of the world around them. Their appreciation for pretty things, inspiring a more careful nature, all because she let them use small Mason jars for their milk. He sighed, wishing he'd seen the simplicity of this sooner.

"You're still using sippy cups, aren't you?"

He flushed. "Aiden likes them."

"Of course he does." Rainey shrugged lightly. "There's no risk involved."

"I only use them in the house and the car. Outside I let him use plastic or paper cups, but he spills a lot."

"Practice makes perfect," she offered over her shoulder as she stirred the pork. "Don't you spill sometimes?"

He saw her point. "Of course. But not on the good furniture. Or the carpet. Usually."

"So if you were eating at the table…" Her smile said she'd made her point.

"Got it. No more sippy cups except in the car."

"Well, let's go to point number two." She set a tray of fresh, raw green beans and cherry tomatoes on the table. "Throw the sippy cups away and give him a regular cup with a straw-friendly lid in the car. Sippy cups are for babies. The kids in school will make fun of him if they see him drinking from one of those."

Luke ran a hand through his hair, wondering why he'd been so blind. And wondering how much Aiden had engineered his own coddling.

"Hey, you did tell me to be honest, right?" Rainey faced him, but let her gaze go to the trio in the living room before bringing it back to Luke.

"Yes."

"And I expect you to do the same in return."

"Except you seem real good at all this. Which is kind of weird, because you were gone for three years."

She breathed deep, then stood still for long seconds as the kids tried to tempt a kitten out from under the couch by wriggling a shoelace. "I had time to think. To pray. To remember all the good lessons my mother tried to teach me. But I ignored them. I knew she felt remorseful because I had no father, and I used that to make her feel guilty. By the time she married Tucker McKinney, I was already a brat. But he was good to me. He adopted me, taught me how to ride and care for horses. How to run a tractor. How to milk cows. How to clean the dairy equipment. How to tell the difference between a finch call and a robin's song."

"He loved you."

She grimaced. "And I still messed up. Being away taught me to appreciate what God has given me. I decided that when I got back, I'd be the best mother I could be." She indicated the living room again. "But in many ways I'm still a stranger to them. They run to my mother and Piper first, understandably. I will do whatever it takes to help them be wonderful, sweet young ladies. And we're going to bring that cute little boy along for the ride."

Rainey had bared part of her soul to him. And it wasn't as if Luke didn't realize why she'd run off three years ago. She'd been threatened by a crooked cop with high-level family connections, and she knew that turning him in would make her a target. And she'd thought the cop had the power to send her back to jail for breaking parole.

Her innocence had been proved. Her name had been exonerated.

But even though she was innocent of the crime she'd done time for, the people of Kirkwood Lake remembered the tough crowd she'd run with in high school. The problems they'd caused. People around here might forgive eventually, but they never forgot. And that was going to make things hard on Rainey.

"Supper's ready."

She broke the moment with a quick, fun whistle that brought the girls running. Aiden turned, surprised. "How did you do that?"

Rainey did it again, one short blast, and the boy raced her way, delighted. "I want to whistle like that!"

"We'll practice," she told him. "But not during supper."

Aiden's eyes surveyed the dishes and he shrank back. "I don't like this stuff."

"Really?" Rainey sat down at one end of the table. The girls hopped into their seats to her right. Luke took the chair opposite her, leaving Aiden the choice of sitting next to his father or Rainey. "Have you tried it?"

His face darkened. "No."

"Pulled pork is one of my favorites, Aiden." Luke picked up a soft, chewy roll and layered it with the barbecued meat. "And yellow rice is delicious."

"I love it so much," Sonya said softly. "My

mommy makes it even better than 'Buela, but I don't say that to 'Buela. It would hurt her feelings."

A tender nature. So gentle, so kind. Luke's heart opened to the little girl on his left. "That's nice, Sonya."

She gave him her typical shy smile, but then glanced at Aiden, wide-eyed. "Aren't you going to eat with us?"

"No."

Luke switched his attention to his son. "But you need to sit down with us while we eat."

"Why?"

"Because it's polite."

Aiden made a mulish face, but pulled out the seat and climbed on it with a thud.

Rainey reached out hands to say grace. Luke took Sonya's hand and reached for Aiden's. His son shrank back in the chair, drew up his legs and stared straight ahead, refusing to acknowledge his father's gesture.

From the corner of his eye, he saw Rainey give a slight shake of her head. Luke understood the silent message: ignore the antics.

So he shifted his attention and turned back as Rainey asked God's blessing.

Luke listened to her soft prayer, heard the smile in her voice as she thanked God for her daughters and her family. But when she asked God to bless him and Aiden, Luke longed to shrug off her words. He and his son were doing fine on their own.

But they weren't, and something in Rainey's prayer said she knew that and longed for his happiness.

"Dorrie, can you pass me the salt and pepper, please?"

"Sure." Dorrie had to hike herself up to reach the shakers, but she did it and then beamed at her mom, pleased with her success.

"Sonya, you don't have to eat a lot of meat, but at least try it, okay?"

"Yes…" Sonya dragged the word out softly. She stared at the bowl, until Luke leaned over.

"May I help you?"

She nodded. "Yes, please."

He served her a tiny spoonful of the meat, then smiled when she piled a large serving of the rice-and-corn dish alongside. "And how about vegetables?" Aiden wouldn't touch anything resembling a vegetable, and Luke had stopped making them, opting to avoid the hassle. As Sonya and Dorrie both took fresh beans and tomatoes for their plates, he saw his mistake. How did kids know what they liked if they weren't encouraged to sample things? He'd tried tempting Aiden, but his son wouldn't budge.

Which means you didn't try hard enough, Luke's conscience scolded. Hillary had told him that an eight-ounce juice box with vitamins gave Aiden all the veggies he needed, so Luke had taken the easy way out.

"Girls, remember, there's cake for dessert if you eat a good dinner."

Aiden's eyes flashed to the kitchen counter. The cake tray sat proudly in front of a set of apple-embossed canisters. He stared at it, then turned back. "I love cake."

Rainey flashed him a smile. "Me, too. But we have to take care of our bodies with healthy foods first, right?" She didn't wait for him to answer, just nodded encouragement as she took some rice. "So if you try a little of everything, you can have cake later."

It took a few seconds, but Luke saw when Aiden got the drift of her sentence. He stared at her, then the cake, then back to Rainey. "I don't get cake?" His chin quivered and his face shuttered in sadness.

"Well, of course you do. If you eat some dinner. Luke, maybe if you put a little bit of everything on Aiden's plate, he can see what he likes and what he doesn't like."

"Sounds like a plan." Luke put a tiny serving of pork, of rice and a few green beans on his son's plate.

The boy's lower lip stuck out, threatening, while the girls munched crisp green beans. "Mommy, these are delicious!" Sonya exclaimed.

"I love them like this." Dorrie waved hers around, a miniature green sword in her hand. "I could eat these all day. Mommy packs them in our lunch box."

"I never thought of not cooking them." Luke lifted his sandwich, keeping his gaze off Aiden and on Rainey, which wasn't exactly a punishment.

"We like them steamed, too," Rainey told him. "I love to grill them. Grilled beans and pork chops is one of my favorite dinners."

"I haven't tried that, either, but I can tell you one thing—" Luke set his sandwich down and met her gaze across the table "—this is the best pulled pork I've ever had. Thank you for making it. It tastes smoked. How did you do that?"

"I grill it lightly before simmering it," she told him. "It's my mother's trick. That way you get the wood-fire flavor, then the tenderness by letting it cook slowly in the oven all day."

"Well, I've been to a lot of the barbecue spots around the lake, and no one has anything as good as this."

Her smile said his words meant something more than a simple compliment, and that made him feel good. But his son was still being a stubborn mule, so Luke would have to cut the evening short and take him home after they finished eating.

Rainey had a different idea, though. When they'd cleaned up the table and put things away, she reached out a hand to the kids. "Let's go say good-night to Beansy and the chickens."

"And the new calves!" Dorrie danced toward the door, then spun around and landed theatrically, arms out. "I love saying good-night to the animals."

"And when we come in we can have cake," Rainey promised.

Aiden scampered off the chair. His eyes brightened. "I love cake!"

"Me, too," she told him as she took his hand. "And I'm going to leave your plate right there on the table. That way if you're hungry when we come in, you can eat supper and then have cake with us. Okay?"

He stared at her, then the plate, then the cake dish on the counter.

He gulped twice and bit his lower lip, but didn't crash to the floor or throw a hissy fit. He turned, shrugged off Rainey's hand and went outside with them, sullen but quiet. That in itself was a welcome change.

"Maybe we should call it a night." Luke spoke the words softly so only Rainey could hear. "Tomorrow's an early start and—"

"And you're afraid if we push Aiden he's going to throw a tantrum to get his way."

"Yes."

"Then let's go for another option," she advised him while the kids raced ahead. "Where common sense and quietly standing your ground win out."

"Won't work."

She raised one shoulder high enough to say she doubted him. "We'll see."

She seemed sure of herself. Why was that? She'd only been around the girls for the first two years of their lives, followed by a three-year sabbatical. Now she was suddenly an expert on child rearing?

She poked his arm. "Stop second-guessing everything."

"You're a mind reader, too?"

"Nope." She didn't look up, didn't smile, but her voice held enough amusement for him to imagine the smile, and the image pleased him. "I just figure that's how you got into this mess, by doubting your instincts. And that's why we agreed to work together. Because we'd balance those doubts with faith."

Faith in her abilities to be a smart parent? Maybe. She was certainly comfortable in the role, and he couldn't help but wonder why.

Faith in the God she thanked for dinner, a supper she made with her own two hands?

Not about to happen.

The three kindergartners dropped to their knees, first petting Beansy the goat, then one of the kittens who'd followed them out of the house.

Serenity bathed him. He was pretty sure the feeling would erode once Aiden realized he really wasn't going to get cake, but for right now? Here with Rainey and the kids?

It seemed like he could have it all, and that felt good.

Chapter Five

By the time they got back to the house, all three kids looked tired. Luke supervised as they washed their hands while Rainey cut the cake. He pretended not to see Aiden's hopeful expression, his clear wish that they'd forget about the plate of food on the table and just serve him dessert.

The girls sat down and Rainey set a slice of melt-in-your-mouth cake in front of each of them.

Luke took the seat he had before and smiled when she gave him a much larger piece; he was pretty sure it still wouldn't be enough.

Then she served up a smaller piece for herself, sat down and raised her fork. Before she took a bite, though, she looked straight at Aiden. "There's plenty more cake, honey. If you want some, hop into your seat and give supper a try."

He stood there watching them eat, looking so sad, so forgotten, that Luke longed to cave in and give him the cake. Do whatever he had to do to make Aiden happy.

But sitting there, he realized that his reactions had created a lot of his son's current problems. What had Jack said? That he had to let the kid grow up?

He'd hated his brother then, but saw the wisdom in his words now, so he turned his attention toward the girls.

"This is so good!" Dorrie stretched out the last two words as she licked the whipped cream frosting off her fork. "Mommy, this is my favorite cake in the whole world. Besides chocolate."

"I'm glad you like it." Rainey smiled at her, then raised her gaze to Luke. "What about you?"

"Not like. Love," he declared. "It's amazing. Are you going to make this for your dairy booth? Because you should."

She stared at him, then grinned and laughed. "That's a perfect idea! What better way to draw a crowd than to use milk cake samples to tempt people? Luke, I owe you. I'll add that to my list tonight. And it's just the kind of thing people will order for the holidays."

He'd pleased her. Seeing her face light up, just for him, made him happy. He started to make a snappy reply, but a movement to his right made him pause.

Rainey shook her head in silent warning, so he ignored Aiden as he climbed into the seat and eyed the food with suspicion. Finally the boy raised his fork, speared some pork and took a tiny bite.

No one paid him the least bit of attention, not even when he tried a few more bites of pork. His eyes widened as he tasted the rice and corn, then started cleaning it off his plate. "That's good stuff!"

"Oh?" Rainey nodded at him with an easy calm. "Great, Aiden, I'm glad you like it. How did you like the pork?"

He made a little face, but didn't fuss. "I almost liked it. I think."

She accepted that with a smile. "The important thing is that you tried it. I'm proud of you, honey."

He smiled across the table at her, then hoisted a bean. "If I eat this, can I have cake with you guys?"

"Yes."

He crunched the bean, then grinned. "Dorrie! I think I love these, too! Dad, can I have these in my lunch sometime? They're so good!"

"Sure, bud." Luke pretended indifference, but he longed to get up and dance around the kitchen, enjoying his success. *Rainey's* success, but he saw how easily she'd handled things, and now he had a kid who liked fresh beans and yellow rice. All because she'd quietly stood her ground.

"Good job, Aiden." Rainey didn't make a big deal out of the success, either. She rose, crossed the room and cut him a little piece of cake. "Here you go, honey. Thanks for eating your supper." She put a hand around his shoulders and gave him a half hug. Seeing her do that made Luke pause.

He couldn't risk loving a woman with emotional issues again. And Rainey came with more baggage than a commercial jetliner. She had no love for cops after what she'd been through, either. But seeing her there, with Aiden, made all things seem possible.

Except they really weren't possible, so he'd better put the lid on his emotions and live in the success of the moment. Seeing his son respond in an acceptable manner meant the world to Luke. And that would be enough for now. "Hey, bud. When you're done with your cake, we've got to hit the road. School tomorrow and we're pushing bedtime already."

"Okay."

Rainey and her daughters walked them to their car a few minutes later. The girls raced around, the cold dew chilling their bare feet. A few katydids click-clacked in the trees above, but autumn's chill had sent the birds packing and quieted most of the bugs.

Luke turned as Aiden scrambled into his booster seat. "Thank you for tonight, Rain. It was wonderful."

"You're welcome. We did well." She met his look and swept the tired boy a quick glance. "Step by step."

"Good night, girls."

"Night, Luke!"

"Bye, Aiden!"

They scrambled into the house, shrieking about their wet feet, and Rainey laughed.

"It will take a quiet bath and a couple of stories to calm them down tonight, but thanks so much for taking them out on the lake with your father. I love working in the store." She shifted her attention to the quaint, red-sided building at the back of the stone drive. "But it's tough to give the girls opportunities when you work weekends."

"Piper always said the same thing. And I'm working next weekend, so maybe you could figure out something fun for the kids to do."

Rainey paused, smiled and looked at him. "How about fun and helpful? And potentially messy?"

"Is it legal?"

She laughed, and he realized she might have taken offense, but didn't. And that made him feel dumb for cracking the joke and relieved that she wasn't hypersensitive.

"Yes. If Zach can cut the pieces for the dairy booth, I can have the kids paint them."

"Paint the booth? The booth that you want to have make a good impression on people?"

She nodded. "Why not?" He faltered and she read him like a book. "You're afraid it will look less than perfect."

Bemused, he frowned, because that's exactly what

he'd been thinking. "I thought you wanted to impress people."

"I want to be accepted." She made the correction quietly. "But not at the cost of leaving the kids out of a fun project. You wait and see. You might be surprised by the end result." She stepped back, allowing him room to get into the car. "Then again, you might just have to buzz your kid's hair to remove the paint."

"Great." Luke turned her way. She backed up two steps, her arms folded over her chest to ward off the deepening chill. He thought of so many things he wanted to say, but it was growing colder and Aiden needed to get home. "Thank you."

She smiled and gave him a short wave. "Back at ya. Bye, Aiden."

"Goodbye, Rainey! I love your cake!"

"Good." She hurried into the house as Luke started the engine, and the sight of her, tall and slim, her long hair flowing down her back, made him long to drink her in.

He couldn't, so he pulled away, angled the car onto Lake Road and headed for his place, on the opposite side of the water. The curved road circled the mile-wide lake. Halfway home he realized two things. First, Aiden was starting to doze in his seat, which meant he might let the tired boy sleep in his clothes that night. And second, Luke couldn't get the image of Rainey McKinney out of his mind.

* * *

"Hey, Luke." Hillary greeted him as he strode into his kitchen late Monday afternoon. "What did you do to this kid over the weekend? He's exhausted."

"Is he?" Luke looked around the corner and saw Aiden in front of the TV, mesmerized by a show that was too young for him, a fact he wouldn't have acknowledged two weeks before. "Did he have homework?"

Hillary shook her head. "They don't give homework in kindergarten. Being there all day is enough for the little ones."

A mental red flag popped up. "I was thinking of getting him some work sheets for after school. I'd rather have him doing that than watching this stuff."

Hillary's expression said he was making a big deal out of nothing. "He's five."

"Almost six," Luke corrected. "I held him back a year because of his separation anxiety, remember? So he's almost a year older than the others in his class."

"I wonder if it's fair to measure a boy like Aiden by others' standards, Luke."

A second red flag waved frantically for attention. He picked his words carefully. "What do you mean, 'a boy like Aiden'?"

"Sensitive. A little overwrought. A child who's been through trauma and survived." She turned to look at Aiden through the kitchen doorway, and her expression said she'd protect the boy at all costs. That brought Luke back to his brother's words. Like it or not, Aiden needed to mature like the rest of his age group. And it was Luke's job to see that it happened.

"He needs to move on. We all do."

Hillary studied him, then nodded. "Oh. I see."

"What?"

She shrugged into her dark blazer, fixed the collar with a quick snap of her fingers, then pointed west, across the lake. "*She* comes along and we have to change everything we've been doing for years. All the things we've done to help him over the loss of his mother…"

"She? You mean Rainey?" Anger and chagrin vied for dominance in Luke. "Rainey is trying to help me, yes. And I'm trying to help her with the girls. These kids have been friends for years and maybe, just maybe, we can keep them from flunking kindergarten if they learn how to adjust better. And I think they already are."

"In two weeks?" Hillary jutted her chin toward her car. "I've been a social worker for nearly nine years. I deal with all kinds of family situations, and I can guarantee you that little good happens in just two weeks."

She was wrong, but Luke refused to carry the argument further. He'd been as much to blame for Aiden's behavior issues as Hillary, more so because he was the boy's father. But seeing the quick results of Rainey's methods, he understood he no longer had a choice. He might have to find a different after-school sitter for Aiden on the days he worked late. "I have to do what's best for Aiden, Hillary. You know that."

"I thought that's what we'd been doing." She challenged him with a cool look that said his words insulted her. Worse, she was probably right to be affronted. "You're letting an ex-con direct your son's life."

"Hey—"

Hillary shook her head and moved toward the door. "I know what the papers said. I know she got herself cleared, blah, blah, blah. But that doesn't negate how she and her buddies caused problems wherever they went. Smoking, drinking, picking on others. And here you are, ready to roll out the red carpet for her as if she's mother-of-the-year material. Are you forgetting how she left those adorable twins for her mother to raise for three long years?"

Luke opened his mouth to speak, but Hillary held up a hand to stop him. "I see her in church every week. And she's beautiful, so I get the attraction. But no matter how sweetly she bows her head, no matter how penitent and contrite she seems, a zebra can't change its stripes, Luke. You might want to think about that."

Hillary pushed through the door, let it bang behind her, and strode to her car, shoulders back, chin up.

"Dad? Why is Aunt Hillary mad at you?"

Luke started to say she wasn't upset, but stopped himself. "Come here, Aiden." The boy complied and he lifted him in a big hug. "We've got to change a few things around here, and Aunt Hillary isn't sure it's a good idea."

"Like the furniture?" Aiden looked around the room, puzzled. "You want to move the couch again? And the chairs?"

"No." Luke sank onto a kitchen chair and cuddled his son, wishing wisdom had come quicker. "I want you to try new things. Maybe do some fun worksheet stuff at home like Dorrie and Sonya do."

"I like those," Aiden told him. "Piper used to give me sheets to do when I was over there."

And if Luke had followed Piper's example, Aiden might have been more prepared to participate in school. But there was no sense treading old water. The time for change was at hand. "It will mean more playing and less TV in the afternoons."

"Like at Grandma's."

Luke smiled, knowing his mother would be relieved that he'd finally come around to her way of thinking. "Yes. Like that."

"Aunt Hillary doesn't like to play, though." Aiden leaned back and his puzzled frown made Luke long to hold tight and let go at the same time. "She works on her computer while I watch TV, and sometimes she'll read me a story."

Another lightbulb moment. Keeping Aiden safely tucked inside meant Hillary could work on her laptop. Or hang out on social media.

Dumb, Luke. Just plain dumb. He massaged his temples, then set his son on his feet and went about making supper. Luke warmed up the chicken his mother had given him the day before and put out a bowl of fresh green beans he'd grabbed on his lunch break. The two of them ate at the table, with the TV turned off.

It felt weird. And quiet.

Too quiet. And as Aiden reached for his hand to say grace, as they had at Rainey's, Luke understood himself a little more. Background noise alleviated the need to talk and interact with others. They could be together, eat together, yet be totally separate because the television was on, drawing their attention.

Aiden touched his hand, waiting, but Luke wasn't going to pretend to pray, even for his son's sake. He squeezed Aiden's hand, smiled and handed him the beans. "I got these special for you today."

"Thanks!" Aiden grabbed a handful for his plate and seemed to leave the idea of grace alone now that they were eating. That suited Luke. He'd prayed as a kid, then doubted as a teen. Then he'd thanked God for his healthy son, and prayed when his wife's illness threatened everything he held dear.

No heavenly aid came forth in those troubled years, and Luke had learned to depend on himself.

He'd been raised to be strong and capable, and that's what his son needed most—a dad who looked out for his welfare. He'd gone a little overboard, but he was determined to fix that now.

He called his mother once Aiden was tucked in for the night. "Mom, I need a favor."

"What's up?"

"I may or may not have fired Hillary tonight."

A short silence ensued, then Jenny asked, "Would a round of cheers be considered over the top?"

Luke frowned. "Along with a serving of humble pie for me. It's not like you haven't been telling me this for a year."

"Why now?"

Leave it to Jenny Campbell to get right to the point. "I've been noticing that when people expect more of Aiden, he delivers. I'm not too late, am I? Have I totally messed him up?"

"No." Her quick reply soothed his concerns, until her next comment. "But you've managed to create a kid who guilts you into coddling him, because he expects that reaction now. It's not going to be an easy fix. He'll act out, you'll question your sanity, and you'll be tempted to give in regularly."

"Great." Luke scowled, unseen. "Sounds like fun."

"*Fun* is only one aspect of parenthood," she replied. "And you'll have more fun once Aiden becomes more self-sufficient. So yes, I'll be glad to watch him after school. He loves it here, and I think Hillary needs permission to find her own path. Her bitterness over Martha's death can't be healthy for anyone. I'm glad you see that."

He should have seen it before. He'd blinded himself purposely, determined to prove everyone wrong, to keep his son safe. Luke's choices had crippled Aiden's emotional growth, but then Rainey came along....

"And bring the girls by again soon," his mother went on. "Your father gets such a kick out of Dorrie, but I think Sonya wins his heart with her quiet ways. Those big, round eyes."

Eyes like her mother's, Luke thought, but he kept that opinion to himself. "Will do. They had a ball. That's all they could talk about last night when I drove them home. And Rainey got Aiden to try three new things. Pulled pork, yellow rice and raw green beans."

"There's a small miracle for you." She choked on the end of her sentence, as if smothering a laugh, and Luke wouldn't have expected anything else. He'd been a dolt, and she was allowed to have the last laugh. "Have the school bus drop him here. I'll be waiting."

"Will do." He called Hillary next, waded through the expected tears, reminded her that she was welcome to visit them and ended the call feeling like a first-class heel. But it was high time to shoulder the blame and the responsibility of parenting.

"Yummy cop approaching," whispered Marly a few days later.

Rainey saw Luke heading her way in full uniform, and felt her heart speed up. Unfortunately, her head brought her to her senses. *No cop wants to be tied to a criminal past like yours, no matter what you've done to clean up your act. Keep that in mind. You agreed to work together for the kids' sake, not yours. Remember?*

She remembered, but it was easy to forget in Luke's presence. Dark sunglasses covered his warm blue eyes. His mouth tipped up in that inviting, country-boy smile, speeding up her pulse. "Luke, hey. How's it going?"

He scratched his left ear, a move she'd noticed the week before, something he did when he was thinking. "I was wondering if you were still okay with having Aiden come here to paint on Saturday, although the forecast calls for rain. I'm working all day, but if you're tied up, I'll have my mother watch him."

"Saturday's fine," she told him. He picked up a shopping basket and filled it with food as they talked. "Zach's setting up sawhorses in the barn, so even though they'll make a mess, it will be in a contained area, so not too bad, right?"

Luke sent her a grin that put her heart into a tail-spin, but she made sure her face stayed calm. She hoped.

"And look at you," she quipped. "Stocking up on fresh veggies. I'm proud of you."

"Are you?" He removed the sunglasses and locked eyes with hers, and something in her rebelled at the very idea of staying calm.

"Yes." She whispered the word, because she couldn't for the life of her take a full breath.

He held her gaze, then sighed and smiled, and the combination made her feel as if anything was possible.

"I'm glad." He spoke softly in turn, as if they were sharing state secrets. He squared his shoulders, gave her a quirked smile and moved on to the bread display. "Looks like you've increased your selection here."

She nodded. "That's part of my problem. I had Ada Sammler supply us with a few extra kinds of bread, and then I had Seb Walker do pastries for us."

"We like to stop by his bakeshop in Jamison," Luke said. "Aiden loves those cream-filled dough-nuts."

"Me, too. But if they don't sell quickly, I lose money. So the downturn in business and the excess product has me at a disadvantage."

"Can you cut the bakery orders for a few weeks?" Her frown made Luke laugh. "I get it. You can be tough where the kids are concerned, but you're afraid to hurt Ada's and Seb's feelings, right?"

"It's easy to laugh when you haven't been persona non grata for years."

Luke made no effort to hide his disbelief. "You're mixing personal with business. You can't do that. You can't *afford* to do that. Call Ada and Seb, tell them you need to short the orders except for weekends, and then maximize them again as customers increase. And they will increase," he promised her.

He made perfect sense and his confidence boosted hers. "I'll do it," she promised. "I felt like a loser, increasing the stock, then whining over lack of sales, but you're absolutely right. I'll swallow my pride and take care of it."

"Good." Luke put a six-pack of cinnamon rolls into his basket alongside an acorn squash, a head of cauliflower and a pack of Testy O'Brien's freshly-smoked bacon. "Was it your idea to carry Testy's stuff?"

Testy O'Brien ran a meat-smoking business in Cattaraugus County. His wide selection was well-known and appreciated in the tri-county area.

Rainey nodded. "I'm acting as a middleman for Testy's full line over the holidays, and we've got a gift basket line that Marly's designing. We'll start displaying them soon so people can plan on them for Thanksgiving and Christmas."

"Great idea. I have friends that moved west and

the things they miss most are Testy's smoked meats, Cuba cheese, Sahlen's hot dogs and Abbott's Frozen Custard."

"It's funny what you miss when you're away." She let her gaze wander the store. Piper had sold a tractor to upgrade the dairy store, and her sacrificial move had resulted in wonders for the business. Until Rainey took over.

"Hey, do me a favor and hold this—" Luke handed her the basket "—while I grab some milk. There's nothing like McKinney Farms chocolate milk in glass bottles."

He tweaked her nose with a swift touch of his thumb, but didn't wait for her reaction as he grabbed a half gallon of chocolate milk and a half gallon of whole milk. He followed that with two dozen eggs, a brick of Cuba cheese, a bag of cheese curds and a pound of butter. "Dairy is an essential food group, I'm told."

"You've been paying attention."

He led the way to the checkout counter and didn't complain when he had to unfold several twenties to cover his purchases, which made Rainey realize something else. Luke could afford all that he'd packed into his baskets because he had a good-paying job with benefits. But what about those who weren't so blessed?

An idea bloomed inside her head, the thought of running a thrift table for people who were down on their luck. Product that would have been wasted would be turned into good food for others. She would run the idea past Piper, but it made perfect sense. Not a handout, but a hand up, and that reasoning worked for Rainey.

Luke pocketed his change, started to hoist the bags with the cheese and milk, then dropped his eyes to the sack of bakery products. "I could use help getting to my car, miss."

Marly laughed behind the counter.

Rainey shot her a scolding look, lifted the bag and started for the door. "Let's go, Deputy. I've got phone calls to make."

He opened the trunk of the running cruiser, set his two bags down, then reached for Rainey's as she moved forward.

His hand closed over hers. She'd walked outside, determined to offer nothing more than a smile and a wave, but the warmth of his palm against the back of her hand made her sigh inside. "Luke."

"Yes, Rain?" The soft question in his voice said he faced a similar problem, one they both needed to avoid.

His hand tightened over hers. He halved the already narrow distance between them, and she was face-to-shoulder with a blue uniform shirt, a badge and pins of commendation.

Too close.

She took a step back, pushing memories away,

wishing she'd been different. Better. Stronger. In Rainey's life, being close to a cop brought up all kinds of bad choices, things she should have done differently.

Stand straight and tall. Hold your head high. Be the example those little girls need.

Away from Luke she could believe Paul's teachings to the Corinthians. His conversion from evil to good had turned Rainey's life around. If a sinner like Saul could turn into a believer named Paul, then she could restart her fractured life.

Luke reached out and touched her chin lightly. She had to look up; there was no other option when his finger grazed her skin. "I'll drop Aiden off on Saturday, okay?"

She nodded because she couldn't trust herself to speak. One word might unleash an entire speech about why they should avoid one another, and right now, the last thing she wanted to do was avoid Luke Campbell.

He climbed into the car, waved and headed to the winding drive leading back to Lake Road. She walked back inside, then held up a hand, staving off any comments Marly might be tempted to make.

Her coworker laughed, anyway. "You know that scene in *Sleepless in Seattle* when Tom Hanks and Meg Ryan come face-to-face on the street?"

"I love that scene," Rainey admitted.

"Well, it has nothing on the one I just saw play out right here, right now. Congratulations, Rainey."

"Marly—"

She backed away, then waved Rainey off. "Customers coming in, and you have stuff to do so I'll say no more...."

"Because you've said enough already," Rainey noted wryly.

"The good thing is I know when to stop." Marly smiled at the customer and dropped a wink in Rainey's direction. "I'll call you if we get busy out here."

Rainey would love that. Last Saturday had been busier than the whole previous weekend, so maybe things would be looking up as Piper had said. But in the meantime Rainey would do everything she could to help. If the store was filled with customers, she wouldn't have nearly so much time to think of Luke Campbell, and that would be good for everyone's sake.

Chapter Six

"Now that's a wonderful aroma," Piper declared as she banged into the kitchen in her usual quick fashion that evening. "Rainey, what are you making?"

"Cinnamon milk to sell for the holidays."

Nose twitching, her sister moved forward. "It smells great."

Rainey made a face. "Well, it's not quite right. I'll get Mama's advice. Don't you have a bicentennial meeting tonight?"

"If by 'you' you mean 'we,' then yes. We have to leave in fifteen minutes, so Lucia will put the girls to bed."

"I'm going?" A combination of dread and aggravation pushed Rainey a step back. "Do you really need me there?"

"Do you want to have your own booth?"

Tonight was the meeting that required all festival participants to present their final plans to the committee, to kick off Kirkwood Lake's year-long bicentennial celebration. And Piper's site plans had been altered to include a separate dairy booth, so the committee might have questions. "I'll go get cleaned up."

Piper glanced down at her farm clothes and grinned. "Me, too."

The town hall conference room had standing-room only by the time Piper and Rainey arrived. Piper squeezed in to the left of the door, acknowledging friends with a quick wave.

Rainey slipped in beside her, but focused on the committee. Most folks would act nice in a public venue, but she wasn't about to chance catching a sour look from someone in the crowd. She needed to be on her game tonight if the committee needed answers.

And they did, once they came to Piper's revised booth layout. "Piper, your site plan has been revised according to the email we received last week?" Tess Okrepcki adjusted her reading glasses, then peered over them to address Piper directly.

"Yes."

"You're doing a farm-products booth and a dairy booth."

"That's right. But within the original site footprint," she added.

"And you have enough product to stock both booths for two days?"

"Yes. The farm booth is a cooperative of McKinney Farms and a few smaller farms that supply us with goods for the fresh foods part of our business. I'll let my sister tell you about the dairy booth."

Rainey turned toward Piper. Piper's look said she had absolute confidence in Rainey's ability to carry the moment. She turned, faced the committee and dived in. "The dairy booth will feature our normal products, but it will also kick off our holiday sales opportunities by showcasing the new line of gift baskets and holiday-specific items we'd like customers to try. At this point we're still developing product lines but we'll be having folks sample *tres leches* cake, cinnamon milk and other new dairy ideas for a long, cold Western New York winter."

"Do you have appropriate electrical setup?"

"We do."

"And backup generator power?"

Piper made a face, but Rainey nodded, confident. "Yes, I do."

"And you know the temperature range for cooling dairy products has to be respected at all times?"

Rainey patted her side pocket. "I have my food handler certification from the state of New York right here."

The committee chairwoman smiled, and Rainey

blessed Piper for making her take the three-day course at the community college before summer ended.

"And you have enough staffing for both booths?"

"Marly Peterson, Julia Harrison Morse and I are handing the dairy booth."

"Marty Harrison and I are on the farm-product booth," Piper added.

"Well, it sounds like you've got the bases covered," the chairwoman said, and for just a moment, Rainey thought they were done.

But then a hand shot up from a seat across the room. The chairwoman nodded her way. "Laura Spelling."

The woman stood, her chin thrust out, her back rigid. "Anyone with a lick of sense knows it's a hazard to have glass bottles on the park grounds. You're just asking for accidents to happen, and if she—" a hooked thumb and a tart tone indicated Rainey "—gets distracted, then we have problems. I, for one, am tired of cleaning up other people's mistakes."

The chairwoman offered the speaker a quiet look of confusion. "Distracted? What do you mean, Laura?"

"Busy." The woman sniffed audibly, then folded her arms across her chest. "When you appropriated space for my 'premium' level booth on the main walk, it was across from McKinney Farms. Now—" she sent a mean-spirited look across the room to Rainey "—it's directly opposite *her*."

"Your booth hasn't been changed, Laura. The McKinneys simply added a separate stand for their dairy store. So really, nothing has changed. Same footprint, same allocation, same traffic flow."

"But it's *not* the same." Laura pulled up her shoulders as if spoiling for a fight. "I didn't pay good money to have a premium stand for my yarn goods and handmade crafts right across from a criminal. That changes a lot, Tess."

Tess looked caught, as if she couldn't believe this was happening.

A movement from the back of the room drew the chairwoman's attention. "Have you got something to say, Luke?"

"I do."

Rainey turned and saw him tucked in the back of the room. She hadn't thought about Luke being here, but he'd mentioned he was running a petting zoo at the festival.

He smiled at her, then at Tess. "I have a premium site for my petting zoo about a hundred yards south of Laura's. If she's so inclined, I'll trade my spot for hers. That way she'll have a prime location for her goods and I'll take the site across from Rainey's."

"Laura." Tess turned back to the yarn-goods dealer. "Will that work for you?"

"Yes." The woman maintained her ongoing displeasure with the possible solution, however. "That means you're putting a draw for children directly across from her booth, but if the committee is okay with that, who am I to say it's a stupid idea?"

It was all Rainey could do to keep Piper from charging across the room. But she held her sister's arm and whispered, "Humility first. Always."

Piper's face said she had other ideas of what Rainey could do with her humility, but then Luke took another step forward in a reassuring fashion. "We won't let the kids or the animals mess with Rainey's stuff. I promise." He gave Laura a nod of reassurance, deliberately misunderstanding her ploy, and then winked at Rainey and Piper. "We'll keep things under control."

Laura snapped her mouth shut and said no more. Seeing her expression, Rainey was sure she hadn't heard the last of it, but Luke had saved the day. As the meeting drew to an end, he moved across the room, his brother Seth at his side. "Ladies."

Piper aimed a mutinous look at Laura Spelling's back. "Vindictive snot."

Rainey shook her head. "She's protecting her investment. I'm paying off past mistakes. That's how it goes, Piper." She turned her attention to Luke. "Thank you."

His grin said more than words ever could. "None needed. I just engineered two days of being within a few feet of you and didn't have to lay out an extra dime. I'd say I'm the winner here."

Rainey shook her head, bemused but gratified,

and stuck out her hand to his brother. "You're Seth. I know this because your picture is in Luke's living room."

"Nice to meet you, Rainey." He shook her hand, then shrugged a shoulder toward the angry woman's retreating back. "You handled that well. I noticed that Piper wanted to go on the attack, but you held back."

"I've learned restraint the hard way," she admitted. "I didn't expect to come home to find an 'all is forgiven' mind-set," she said, as the crowd thinned. "But I didn't know it would be as bad as it is."

"Oh, Rainey." Piper hugged her. "It will get better with time."

"It will," she agreed quietly. "I pray for that every morning. And every afternoon. And then double-time in the evening, because I know that actions have repercussions. I just want God to give me the strength to handle those waves when they come."

"Well, Zach and I are arranging security throughout the bicentennial year," Seth told her. "Between the three of us—" he gave his younger brother a punch in the arm "—we've got your back."

"Thank you, Seth." She smiled up at him. "That means a lot."

"To *both* of us," Luke advised his brother. "And I'll be glad to let you know when your help is needed." His direct look sent a message that made Seth smile.

"Got it."

"Good. Did you girls walk down?"

Piper shook her head. "We were running late, so we drove. And, Luke, thank you again." She reached out and hugged him. "You're a good friend."

He turned Rainey's way with a look of expectation. "No hug?"

She frowned and tapped his chest lightly. "Rules, remember?"

"You won't let me forget." His amused but wounded glance said he'd like to set the rules aside.

"Then it's good that one of us is paying attention." She slid into the passenger seat of the car, fastened her belt and waved. "Thanks, guys."

"You're welcome." Seth's voice followed her, amused.

"See you Saturday, Rain." Luke's tone sounded determined, as if the man had made up his mind to challenge the guidelines they'd set weeks before.

The thought of thwarting those rules tempted Rainey's heart. What would it be like to give this relationship a chance to grow?

You left your children for years, you've just come home, now you're contemplating changing things up again? What's wrong with taking things slow? Step by step? Wasn't that your plan?

But what if God's plan included Luke and Aiden?

Laura Spelling's look of revulsion came back to her, a woman so disgusted with Rainey's past that she didn't want her in her field of vision, afraid she would taint her business.

The phone was ringing when they walked into the house. Rainey picked it up without looking at the number, then slapped it back down quickly.

"Telemarketer?" Piper frowned as she tossed her jacket onto the back of a chair. Then she turned Rainey's way. "Not a telemarketer."

Rainey bit back tears, determined to stay strong. "Laura wanted me to know what she really thinks of me in words she didn't dare use in public."

"Are you kidding me?" Piper asked, steaming. "Rainey, you paid your price and then some. You never even committed a crime. And Laura threw her kid out of the house because she discovered she was pregnant last year. The church and the ladies' auxiliary have been helping support Laura's daughter and granddaughter because Laura disowned them. You want to talk sinful behavior? That's it right there. I will never understand hypocritical behavior like this."

Rainey understood too well. "Guilt by association. It's simple. It takes a lot of good things to build a solid reputation, and one bad thing can ruin it. I messed up repeatedly, so I've got a lot of work to do to scrape off the tarnish. But I'm tough." She stared at the phone. "And people like Laura Spelling should take a lesson in forgiveness."

"But it's not your fault," Piper insisted, indignant.

Rainey gave her a tired smile as she headed for bed. "This time, yes. But I'll be trudging uphill for a while, Piper. Luckily I've got some good shoes on my feet."

Chapter Seven

Luke dropped Seth at his rustic village house in Kirkwood before he headed home on the far side of the lake. The dark front windows said his mother had tucked Aiden in for the night. He stepped into the kitchen and took a deep breath of anticipation. "Lasagna."

"Seth called and said you were on your way, so I warmed it up." Jenny grabbed a jacket from a hook beside the door and shrugged into it while she talked. "Aiden ate a little, not too much, but he did wolf down fresh green beans and cottage cheese."

"He's discovering new things every day."

"Seth mentioned some trouble at the meeting."

"Yes." Luke withdrew a fork and knife from the drawer and moved to the table. "Folks aren't making things easy for Rainey."

"Evening up the score." Jenny frowned at the thought. "If we all minded our own business, the world would be a better place. Or if we looked out for one another."

"Rainey thinks she deserves it."

"She's wrong." His mom's expression matched her quick tone. "She made mistakes when she was a kid. Most people understand that and move beyond. Laura Spelling is always looking to assign blame, and it's never at her own front door."

"I moved the petting zoo across from the Mc-Kinneys' stand," Luke told her. "Unless Seth already filled you in."

Her nod said he had.

"It's better that way, anyhow," Luke went on. "We want the kids to feel like they're helping with the festival, so if we've got a crew of adults around, that will make it easier to let them work here and there."

"I won't be much help to you that weekend," she reminded him. "Dad and I are working with the fire department booths and the ladies' auxiliary pumpkin pull."

"We'll be fine. The kids are painting the boards for Rainey's booth this weekend."

Jenny raised a brow in approval. "Luke, I'm proud of you. You're giving Aiden a chance to breathe on his own. Well done."

Luke couldn't argue the point, because he had his mouth full of lasagna, the best food he'd had all day. "This is awesome." He mumbled around a forkful, and she waved as she walked out the door.

"Luckily, Aiden and I said grace for all three of us."

"Yeah, yeah." Luke waved at her retreating back. "You pray enough for half a dozen Campbells, Mom. And I know you've got my back."

She turned at the door and her look reminded him of all those times she'd been right when he was a kid. "God's got your back, son. But I've got Him on speed dial as needed. Good night."

"Night. And thanks again for watching Aiden."

She waved and climbed into the small SUV she used for tooling all over their mountainous county, and Luke sat back, contemplating her words.

God had his back?

Not likely. Never had, never would. But as Luke finished the plate of delicious, hot food, Rainey's words came back to him, how she prayed morning, noon and night. The image of a young mother bowing her head in prayer made him pause.

His wife, Martha, had never taken charge of things. And she'd never talked about prayer, even though she insisted on going to church each Sunday.

He was ashamed to admit he'd been married to the woman and didn't know if she prayed or not. How crazy was that? And he'd gone to church with her, but because he was supposed to be there. The Campbells had all been raised in the church, steeped in faith, then allowed to find their own way.

"Oh, ye of little faith." Rainey had used that expression on him the week before, and he'd sloughed it off, thinking it was just another phrase. But it wasn't, not to her, and not to his mother or father.

He stood, loaded his plate and silverware into the dishwasher, and stared at the night sky. Encroaching clouds promised rain by morning, enough to make the farmers groan during harvest. But the dark skies had nothing on the shadows in his heart.

Puddles dotted the farm drive as Luke headed toward the dairy store parking lot late Saturday afternoon. He'd dropped Aiden off that morning, dressed in old clothes, perfect for painting. And when he'd said goodbye before going to work, Aiden had barely acknowledged him.

Which was good, right?

You want him to stop clinging. Isn't that the goal here? To give him wings?

Yes, but Luke couldn't deny the hint of loss he'd felt as he drove away. Aiden didn't need his father, not as much, anyway. But that was Luke's problem, not his son's. He pulled to a stop under a wide-branched maple tree, ready to see what the day had brought.

Piper headed his way as he exited the car. Zach was lighting the grill behind his house next door. Through the dairy store window, he saw Rainey taking care of customers.

What he didn't see were the children.

He moved toward Piper. "Are the kids in the house with Lucia?"

"They're in the barn," she explained. "Cleanup time."

"With Berto."

Piper shook her head as Rainey came through the door of the dairy store. "No, Berto and Marty are in the milking parlor."

"Then who's with the kids?"

Piper hesitated, then addressed his question in a slow, overly careful voice. "No one. I left them on their own to rake up the straw we used under the painting project, but I made sure to spread freshly sharpened pitchforks around first. After I left the keys in the tractor, of course. And the gate to the bull's pen is wide-open, but they'd never venture in there, right?" She scowled and crossed her arms. "What's your deal, Luke?"

"My deal is you left my kid alone in a barn filled with dangerous animals, tools and a ladder to the loft."

Piper didn't shrink back, but then, she never did. Usually Luke liked that about her, but not today.

Rainey stared at him as if he'd grown two heads in seven short hours. "Come with us." She and Piper led the way to the barn, and Luke tried to calm down, but the thought of Aiden alone, possibly in trouble, with no one around…

He felt as if someone had grabbed hold of his heart. What if—

"Hey, Dad!"

"Luke! Come see what we did!"

"Hi."

Sonya blinked up at him with fawnlike eyes while Dorrie jumped up and down and Aiden pumped his fist in the air. "We got all the boards painted and next week Rainey is going to let us put stickers on them!"

There wasn't going to be a next week, Luke decided, but he'd tackle that later. Right now he wanted to grab his kid and hit the road.

"Come on, Dad." Aiden put his hand in Luke's, but not to be led. No, this time, Aiden was leading, tugging his father to the side wall. "These are the boards. Zach put them over here to dry when we got them done."

"They're beautiful," Luke told him. They were anything but beautiful, but they were painted white, looking fresh and clean, and the splotches of paint would do no harm once dry. "Good job, guys."

"Thanks!" Aiden went to pull away, but Luke held tight, ready to go before he exploded. "We need to head home, son."

"Dad, I have to stay," Aiden insisted. "It's cleanup time, and Rainey said we don't get ice cream if we don't help with cleanup."

Aiden was begging to help, a welcome change.

The boy's earnest look pushed Luke to let go of his hand. "Okay."

Aiden dashed back to grab his child-size rake, and he and the girls made a show out of gathering the straw, then piling it into the wheelbarrow. Luke sighed, glanced around, then realized two sets of cool, indignant eyes were trained on him.

Right then, he didn't care.

"As you can see, there are no dangerous tools." Piper drawled the last two words, letting him suffer at length. "No wild animals, ready to eat small children."

"And please make note of the hay pile at the bottom of the ladder, because we did ladder climbs and hay jumps earlier and your sweet baby boy loved it." Rainey's cool, clipped tone said she didn't appreciate his implication of neglect any more than her sister did.

Luke noted the distance from the floor to the loft above. Twice the distance Aiden climbed to his tree house. The loft had a fence rail running the full length, except for the ladder area, and the tall pile of hay at the base made him think of simpler times. Childhood play at his uncle's farm outside of Olean. He'd loved going there, romping with his farm cousins. And they'd had the occasional bump and bruise, a few stitches here and there, but they'd survived. Thrived, even.

"Now you can either stow your wounded ego and

stay for supper, or go home. But Aiden's earned an ice cream and he should get it." Rainey met and held Luke's gaze, and he realized that when it came to criticism of her mothering skills, the lady in question didn't take it lightly. "Your choice."

"We'll go."

"Fine."

"Fine."

The sisters spoke in unison, one fair, one dark, yet united by the stupidity of his overreaction. But then neither one of them had gone through the emotional tangle he'd endured with Aiden's mother, so they—

"How we doin'?" Zach came into the barn, sensed something amiss and stopped. "What's going on?"

"Luke and Aiden won't be staying for supper." Piper made the statement calmly, but Aiden overheard her and stopped cleaning.

"But Zach's making us hot dogs. And Rainey made a bean thing I might like."

"We'll have supper at home, Aiden."

The little boy stared, then stuck out his lower lip. "I don't want to go home. I want to stay and have supper with Sonya and Dorrie."

"Not this time." Luke saw Zach send a questioning look to Piper, but she shrugged it off in a "later" gesture.

Rainey crossed the barn and knelt by Aiden's side. "How about if I put some of that bean salad in a container to take with you, and you let me know what you think of it next time you see me?"

"I can't stay?" Aiden's pleading tone begged her to offer a different answer, but Rainey shook her head.

"When Dad says you've got to go, you've got to go, right? Didn't we talk about this, guys?" She swept the three kindergartners a look, and each one nodded in turn. Rainey smiled and hugged Aiden close for just a minute, then tweaked his baseball cap. "I didn't know we were going to practice the lesson quite this soon, but I'll see you later this week at school, and then Saturday we'll decorate the booth with the cow stickers. It will be our first official 'sticker party.'" She didn't look at Luke, didn't even acknowledge him with a glance. Focused, she kept her attention fully on the children.

Aiden reached up and hugged Rainey. Then he proceeded to hug Dorrie and Sonya, and Luke's chagrin increased even more when the kid hugged Piper and Zach, too.

"Ready?" The question came out gruffer than Luke intended, but he was already acting like a jerk, so what difference did it make?

Aiden met Rainey's encouraging look, nodded, but didn't pretend to be happy. "I guess."

"Let's go."

"Okay."

Aiden trudged to the car, not arguing, fighting,

pouting or whining, a huge and positive step. When Luke reached into the backseat, Aiden waved him off. "I can do my own belt, Dad. Rainey showed me."

With a long sweep of his arm, the boy pulled the belt out and around his middle, then clicked it into place. And when Luke attempted to cinch the belt tighter, Aiden's hands beat him to it.

"Let me guess. Rainey taught you that, too."

He nodded. "She said we were practicing to be indi…indi…"

"Independent."

"Yes." Aiden smiled that his father got it finally, but Luke's heart grew more sour by the moment. He'd freaked out over the kids being allowed to work and play in the barn.

Luke's father often said that his biggest gift to his children had been teaching them to get along without him.

Rainey was quietly teaching a similar concept to Aiden, encouraging him to try new things. And what did Luke do in return?

Turn tail and run.

He pulled into a fast-food place on Lower Lake Road, ordered a hot-dog kid's meal and saw Aiden's look of surprised confusion in the rear seat. "We couldn't eat hot dogs with Sonya and Dorrie, but we're buying them here?"

Luke didn't have to look any further than his reflection in the mirror to realize the boy's assessment made more sense than the father's. Luke had jumped to conclusions, overreacted and gone off on a tangent because he'd let old buttons get pushed.

Piper was ticked at him.

Zach probably thought he was nuts, and then there was Rainey. She felt sorry for him, but worse, she felt sorry for Aiden.

And the worst part of all?

She was right.

Chapter Eight

Luke tried to get hold of Rainey the following day. Lucia answered the phone and politely said she'd pass on the message.

He called again Monday morning, knowing the dairy store was closed until noon, but Berto said Piper and Rainey were having dress fittings for the upcoming wedding.

Luke ended the call, took a seat in his cruiser and wondered if he should keep trying. His head said no.

His heart said otherwise.

He'd hurt her by not trusting her with his son. Instead of thinking, he'd reacted. Cops couldn't afford the luxury of unplanned action, but when it came to Aiden, his academy training went out the window. He needed to fix things. But how?

Saturday.

He needed to trust her to care for Aiden on Saturday, even though it might be the last thing she wanted to do. She'd invited the boy. Surely she'd still welcome him to the sticker party, even if Luke's presence wasn't requested.

He pulled into the crushed-stone parking lot late Wednesday and spotted Rainey as she turned the key in the lock of the dairy store. Marly saw him, whispered something, then backed away with a wave and smile. She got into her patched-up car and headed home, leaving Luke and Rainey alone.

Rainey turned toward Luke and planted a polite smile on her face, not realizing he'd gotten so close.

Very close.

Close enough for her to see the cloudless blue of his eyes, the wave of his dark blond hair, the strong jaw and late-day stubble. She went to step back, create distance between them, but her heel caught the edge of the wooden step.

"Easy."

Strong arms prevented her fall. Strong arms belonging to a man whose doubting nature made her question herself, and she couldn't allow that to happen. Not after all her hard work. She'd stand tall and strong—and alone if need be. But no matter what, no one was allowed to bring her down. Not ever again.

"You okay?" Concern deepened his voice, made it husky, and his eyes were questioning. Eyes a girl could lose herself in… For just a moment, safe in the circle of Luke's arms, she longed to relax into the here and now.

"Fine, thanks." She pulled back, but his arm resisted her movement. "If you'll—

"I don't think so, Rain." He whispered the words as his mouth found hers in a sweet, gentle kiss that offered too much and promised too little. But she didn't want to pull away. She wanted to linger in the present, forget the past and ignore the future.

"Mom? Are you done at the store? We're ready for story time!"

"I—"

"Rain, I—"

"Don't." She put the flat of her fingers against his mouth. "That shouldn't have happened."

"I disagree. And if you can forgive me for being a first-class jerk the other day, Aiden would like to come for the sticker party. If I didn't spoil everything, that is."

Rainey's gaze lingered on his face, his hair, his eyes, before she stepped back. "You can't spoil something that doesn't exist." She waved a hand between them. "We made rules for a reason."

"And if that reason no longer applies?"

"It does apply." She moved around him and down the two steps, then turned back. "Nothing erases the past, Luke. Can you imagine how angry and protective you'd feel if someone came along and said hurtful things to Aiden because you were with me?

He's an innocent child, and if you've got reservations about letting him loose to play on his own, I can't imagine how you'd feel the first time someone makes him cry because his father's hanging out with an ex-con."

"Rainey—"

She quickly headed toward the house as Dorrie's voice called again. "Saturday is fine. And if you're not working, you're welcome to stand guard. Oops, I mean, hang out."

Would her comment anger him?

It didn't. Rueful, he clapped a hand to the back of his head and nodded. "Saturday. First thing. And then one week until the wedding. Will you save a dance for me?"

"Maids of honor have no time for dancing. We're too busy taking care of the bride, but thanks for thinking of me."

That was all he'd been doing lately. Thinking of Rainey. Morning, noon and night. He drove to his parents' home on the lake, and another round of guilt hit when he saw how tired Aiden was.

"Luke." His mother looked up when he came through the back door. "I was just going to take him home to bed. Sorry I couldn't be at your place with him today, but the washing machine repairman didn't come until late afternoon. Although the irony of being married to the owner of a hardware store and calling a repairman should not go unnoticed."

His father winked at Luke. "And if I could figure out a way to be in two places at once, that would be fine. Think of it as aiding the local economy."

"To the tune of nearly two hundred dollars," Jenny announced, but she gave his dad's hair an easy ruffle as she walked by. "Luckily, it gave Aiden and me a chance to see how repairmen work."

"A teachable moment."

"Have you been reading or is that another Rainey-ism?" Jenny asked.

"Rainey."

"I'm missing those little girls," Charlie announced from the recliner. "Why don't you bring them around Sunday for the family birthday shindig?"

"That's a great idea." Jenny turned back toward Luke. "Ask her, Luke. See if she and the girls are available."

After she'd brushed him off tonight, Rainey would most likely say no, but Luke wasn't about to go into details with his parents. A guy had to cling to some shred of dignity. "I'll ask, but she might be working."

"They alternate Sundays," his mother said as she packed a sandwich for him to take home. "I usually stop in to stock up after church, and she's only there every other one. But I know they switch up sometimes."

His mom's open look didn't fool Luke. She liked

Rainey. It was clear in her gaze, her tone, her invitation. Jenny Campbell always cheered the underdog, she loved the Christmas tree in *A Charlie Brown Christmas* and she wasn't afraid to champion an unpopular cause. Right now the unpopular cause was her son, but she didn't know that.

Had the kiss ruined things? Luke had no idea, but he knew it was unforgettable, and if he'd had a hard time pushing Rainey from his thoughts before, it was nearly impossible now. "Hey, bud. Can you get your coat?" he asked Aiden.

Charlie tossed his grandson the jacket from the foot of his chair. "Need help with the zipper?"

"Nope." Aiden fumbled and worried his bottom lip as he worked the zipper mechanism, but once he got it locked in, he pulled down tight with one hand and up with the other. "I can do it myself."

"Excellent!" Jenny handed him a miniature candy bar. "This is for working so hard to be independent. I'm proud of you."

"Thanks, Grandma!" He grabbed his backpack and ran to the car, climbed in and worked his straps into place without a word of complaint.

"I don't know or care about whatever else might be going on...." Jenny turned to Luke with a pleased expression. "But whatever you and Rainey are doing seems to be working. He's becoming much more self-reliant and less sulky."

Luke gave credit where it was due. "Rainey, mostly."

"Tell her to keep up the good work. I'll tell her myself if she comes along on Sunday. I've never seen Aiden so anxious to do well. It's an answer to my prayers, Luke."

"Which means Rainey's the answer to your prayers." He started to leave, then turned back. "Though most of the town would disagree."

"Not most. Some," Jenny replied. "That will happen anywhere. But kids make mistakes. That girl had the courage to take someone's place in prison to save an unborn child being born behind bars. She turned in a band of dirty cops and her whistle-blowing brought down a multi-county drug ring. I'd say she's one amazing young woman, but then I like girls who think for themselves."

"I wonder why," his father muttered from across the room.

Luke laughed, but saw the truth in her words. Rainey did think for herself. She'd said so the day they'd met and then proved it in multiple ways. Where Piper dived into a problem, Rainey quietly assessed, then took charge. Luke liked that about her. "I'll ask her about Sunday."

"Good."

"And about the babysitting, I keep meaning to put an ad in the paper, but—"

His mother waved that off. "Why not leave things as they are for the moment? Between the festival and the holidays, we're going to be busy. When did you think you'd have time to interview people? And starting a new sitter at holiday time probably isn't the best idea."

"Time's a problem," Luke admitted.

"So leave it alone for now, let Aiden continue to come here after school and we'll tackle it after Christmas. If that's okay with you."

"It's great. You're sure you don't mind?"

"Wouldn't offer if I did," she told him. "Now go. Get that kid home. I'll see you tomorrow."

"G'night, Mom." He reached out and hugged her, knowing if he didn't she'd chase him down. No one put Jenny Campbell off easily. Most didn't bother trying. "Good night, Dad."

"See ya," Charlie called from his recliner.

Luke got Aiden tucked into bed with half a story, then laid out clothes for the morning. Grabbing a lined flannel shirt, he walked the perimeter of the barn to check the animals. Once he decided all was well, he looked up at the clear night sky and sighed.

Ten years ago he'd envisioned a different reality. He'd started his marriage as a "probie" in cop terms. Year by year he'd built a reputation, a place in the community.

It had all come crashing down after Aiden's birth. Everything he'd had dissolved into a puddle of emotional upheaval.

He'd prayed then. Tirelessly. Endlessly. He'd gone to church, lit candles, sat in the pew like the good

Christian his mother had raised him to be, knowing his world was turning inside out and he was helpless to stop it.

But God could help. He'd believed that then. And when no help came, he realized that the comfort of church was the communal meeting, not the Everlasting Father. Because if there was such a being, He'd have stepped in. No merciful God would ever have put a kid in that position, therefore He couldn't exist.

But standing there under the sky, a blanket of flickering lights, Luke thought of the lessons he'd learned as a child. Christ the teacher, explaining His father and His father's purpose. To love, shelter and forgive.

Christ the healer. The miracle worker. The sage who called the little children to come to Him, stand by Him.

But Luke had no real answers. Just more questions. Because in his world, God should be the greatest protector of all, the "megacop," the enforcer. And when Luke had needed Him most, He hadn't been around. And that made believing not just hard. It made it impossible.

"Okay, sample time." Rainey passed out tiny cups of ice-cold cinnamon milk at the Friday-night farm meeting. "Blended, pasteurized, homogenized, packed in chilled twelve-ounce bottles. What do you think?"

She studied the group as they tasted, then breathed relief at the circle of smiles. "Worthy to sell?"

"Wonderful," Lucia told her. "And the perfect balance of sweet to spice. The price?"

When Rainey quoted the figure, Piper whistled. "A little high, but in line with chocolate milk and less pricey than eggnog. And you brought Testy in on this?"

"For the maple syrup," Rainey explained. "Most places use honey, but I didn't like the aftertaste. The maple syrup will please folks, it's locally produced and it's a perfect match for cinnamon."

"It's a winner," Marty announced. "What's next, and please tell me it's whatever I see in those dessert cups on the counter."

Rainey laughed and nodded as she procured the tray. "*Tres leches* cakes. The pink cups are the traditional recipe, the blue cups are the apple-eggnog variety for the holidays, and the bright yellow are the tropical version, a blend of coconut and pineapple."

Lucia's brows shot up at that, and Rainey wondered if she'd offended her mother by changing the basic family recipe. But when Lucia tasted the tropical cake, she beamed. "I have never had better."

"Really?" Lucia's approval made Rainey grin with delight. "I kept testing varieties on Marly and Uncle Berto. Uncle didn't mind a bit." She winked at him as he patted his rounded middle. "But Marly threatened to charge the store for a weight-loss program if I didn't stop. Still, she gave her approval to these three."

"Well, she's right." Zach reached for a second sample of the apple eggnog version. "This is amazing. I'm not a coconut fan so that one wouldn't tempt me, but this?" He reached out to bump knuckles with Rainey. "You crushed it. This has just become a new holiday favorite."

"Sweet!" She laughed and checked out her sister's opinion.

"No complaints here," Piper told her. "They're marvelous. How are you going to get them ready for the festival, though?"

Rainey whipped out a printed schedule from her left hip pocket. "Baking on Monday and Tuesday. Then I'll freeze the sponge cakes. We fill them Thursday and Friday while the guys set up the booths. The cinnamon milk will be blended and bottled on Thursday. Marly and Noreen will be there to help get things ready. And I'm thinking of little custard cups, too, but I'm not sure if I have the time to pull it off. Those might have to wait until next year. We'll see. We've done up sample Christmas baskets for display. I'm carrying Testy's smoked meats in the cooler—"

"His peppered bacon makes a guy wonder why he ever eats anything else," Zach noted.

Rainey smiled. "It's great, right? So that's it

for now, besides the usual. The eggnog, milk and flavored milks will all be in twelve-ounce bottles with easy-open tops, an alternative to pop and cider for folks grabbing food at the festival. I've decided not to haul the big stuff, because it's awkward to carry half gallons to a park. Instead, I'm focusing on building awareness, availability and affordability. And on that note…" She turned to Piper, her mother and Marty. "I was thinking of starting a thrift table in the store. Half-priced items about to go out-of-date. What do you think?"

Piper exchanged looks with Marty and shrugged. "It's a great idea and I'm wondering why we didn't think of it before."

"I like it," said Lucia. "Rainey, what a good idea."

"Okay, done." She stepped back, pleased with their combined reactions. "That's it for my presentation tonight, but I'm so glad you guys approve."

"Oh." Zach sent her a lazy grin as he reached for another dish of cake, right behind his father and Berto. "We approve. Wholeheartedly."

"Do you need help with the baking schedule?" Piper asked, but Lucia shook her head.

"If Rainey doesn't mind, I will work on the baking while she makes sure the filling is done her way on Thursday. And we'll clear out the big back cooler to store the *leches* cakes. Milk cake is all the better for sitting a day or two."

"Thanks, Mama."

"It is my pleasure," Lucia answered, and the way she said it, as if it *was* a pleasure, strengthened Rainey's resolve. She could do this.

You must do this, her conscience scolded. *There is a difference.*

Maybe, thought Rainey, but seeing the ring of appreciative faces deepened her insight. She wanted to please these people, her family. She longed for their blessing, their approval, even if it was over something as simple as milk and cake. Those smiling faces meant the world to her.

Awkward? Not awkward?

Luke weighed the question as he pulled into the McKinney Farms parking lot on Saturday morning. Aiden craned his neck to see who was outside, then yelled to the girls when they raced out of the wide barn opening to greet him.

Piper strolled behind the girls, and the look on her face said Luke had better be on his best behavior today, or else. He knew better than to mess with a bride one week before her wedding.

"Good morning. We came to do stickers," he called politely.

She pointed to the larger barn with an overhang to her left. "You're on picnic-table duty. We need those tables lightly sanded and painted so that my wedding guests don't get splinters next week."

"Won't it be hard for people to slip in and out of picnic tables wearing dresses and suits?" Luke asked.

Piper's expression said it couldn't be helped. "It's mostly locals and country people, so I'm hoping they'll be fine with these. Renting tables and chairs is crazy expensive and Marty has already done too much. And we've got those portable tables up there." She pointed toward the farmhouse front porch. "Lucia's using them today to serve lunch, but we'll have them for the wedding, too."

"Sounds fine to me." Luke understood her family pride, so he nodded, ready to help, then glanced around, hoping to see Rainey.

Not a glimpse.

He buried his disappointment, waved goodbye to Aiden and jogged over to the wide barn doors.

"More help. Good." Zach handed him an electric sander armed with medium-grade paper and a set of earplugs. "I should have had you bring Seth along. We could use another set of hands. My hope is to beat the rain."

"He's off today. I'll phone him." Luke called his brother, spoke briefly, then turned back to Zach. "He's on his way."

"How do you two manage to have the same weekends off?" Zach wondered.

Luke lifted a shoulder as he scanned his first table for rough spots. "My mother's request. She feels better about us both being deputies if we've got each other's backs."

"That's lovely, Luke."

Rainey.

He turned, wanting to make sure she didn't hate or mistrust him. Maybe even see a glint of happiness in her eyes, reflecting his emotions.

But she kept moving, up the steps and into the dairy store, the screen door slapping shut behind her.

Zach's laugh said Luke wasn't fooling him, but Luke refused to make eye contact. If he sanded long enough and hard enough, maybe he'd forget she was two hundred feet away, taking care of customers in the quaint store.

"Food break."

Smoke-gray eyes met his nearly three hours later. The team of men had lightly sanded, wiped and painted a dozen tables. Moose Braeburn had come over to help from a neighboring farm, Marty took two hours off from the harvest, and Vince Hogan, a neighbor from up the road who'd just sold his farm to Marty and Piper, stopped in, as well.

Rainey motioned to the buffet table on the porch. "You guys must be starving. Mama made breakfast sandwiches, latkes, stuffed sugared pancakes, and there are samples of the cakes I'm serving at the festival for dessert."

Did her eyes linger on Luke longer than anyone else?

No.

Did she sneak a surreptitious glance his way?

Not even a tiny one.

Was he about to go stark raving mad?

Absolutely.

But he wasn't about to acknowledge his problem. He washed up, made sounds of appreciation over the food and followed her lead. If she could be this adept at ignoring him, he could do the same. She was simply following the rules she'd set originally. Nothing wrong with that, right?

They gathered to eat around the folding tables on the porch. Piper and the children joined them, but the kids refused to sit. Instead they ran about, nibbling bits and pieces, then tore off to visit the dwarf goat, the baby calves and the pup that lived next door.

And except for Rainey ignoring him, it felt... good. Natural. Like a Campbell gathering, with folks here, there and everywhere, kids romping and screeching, having the time of their lives.

"Hey."

His heart skipped a beat as Rainey slipped into the seat next to him. "Hey, yourself. I thought you were ignoring me."

She sent him a cool, amused look. "Deputy, despite your inflated yet adorable ego, it isn't always about you." She gave the dairy store a quick glance. "I have a business to run, milk to process, and I work on Saturdays, so if your male ego took a burn because I wasn't on hand to admire your handiwork, let me fix that now." She waved her bottle of tea toward the tables and offered a salute. "Awesome job, Luke. And Seth, Moose, Vince and Zach. They're beautiful and wedding-worthy."

"And you won't have to fancy them up for next year's ice cream season," Luke noted.

She turned his way and nodded, then held her hand up to bump knuckles with him. "Perfect, right?" She touched her fist to his in a show of friendly solidarity. "We'll stow them after the wedding and be ready for spring. Being ahead of the game is never a bad thing around here. And I'm hoping Mother Nature gets all this rain out of her system this week, leaving us a beautiful sunny weekend for the wedding. Otherwise I will spend my one day off this week cleaning the barn."

She stood to go, but he reached out a hand to stop her. "We're having a family thing at my parents' place tomorrow and I wondered if you and the girls would like to come."

"I, uh—"

"I checked with your mother and she said you're not working, and it's scheduled for midday, so after church is perfect. Say yes and I'll let you get back to work. The girls love coming to my parents' place."

"So they said."

"And you can meet my family."

Her eyes darkened slightly, and he read the hint of apprehension. He squeezed her fingers gently. "It will be fine. I promise."

She should say no. She knew it. He knew it. But the look on his face, his hopefulness, matched hers, so she nodded and pulled her fingers free. "Yes."

"Yes? Good."

"What time should we come?"

"I'll pick you up at one."

"No, Luke, we can drive. I'll—"

He held her gaze, and the gentle intensity of those blue eyes kept her in place, her heart beating a mile a minute. "I'll be here at one."

"Okay."

He reached out a hand to hers again, a featherlight touch, a gesture that called her closer.

Her heart softened, seeing his look. Reading his emotions. Growing, just like hers.

"Rainey?" Marly's voice broke the spell.

"Duty calls." Rainey hurried back to the store, eager to be away but unwilling to leave, a clutch of emotions tight in her chest. When she got to the door, she turned and saw him watching. Waiting. Hoping she'd turn.

And she had.

And if she hadn't fallen for Luke Campbell before, she did then.

Chapter Nine

The Cosgrove family had changed pews. So did the Appletons.

They had migrated to the far right, not far from Laura Spelling. Piper's low hum said she was holding back a storm of displeasure. Lucia and Berto seemed unaware as they filed in behind her.

Rainey couldn't help but notice. She kept her eyes trained ahead, refusing to concede the change with a glance around. *Help me, God. Help me to stand tall, not proud. I'm nervous. This whole thing with people's rejections makes me tense inside. And now going to meet Luke's family? His parents? Help me to be the kind of woman You want me to be, and to accept what happens with grace and dignity.*

A woman came through the right-hand side door and walked back a dozen pews.

Hillary Baxter, Aiden's aunt.

She took a seat in front of Laura Spelling, next

to the Cosgroves and behind Mrs. Appleton. They formed a contingent in their corner, while Rainey sat in the now less populated section on the left.

If Luke's sister-in-law had joined forces against her, why was Rainey going to a family gathering today? More derision? More ridicule? Would Luke intentionally set her up for that?

No.

But even a lawman had only so much power, and sensing the negativity rising from those pews, Rainey felt her heart tighten. Luke Campbell tempted her to trust change. To believe that people could change.

Not all, Luke. And maybe not enough.

She wrapped an arm around Dorrie's shoulders while Sonya pored over a small picture book about Jesus calling the fishermen to help teach God's love. So different despite their identical genetics, and so dear. She couldn't take them away from the people they'd loved from birth, and that meant her new start had to be here in Kirkwood Lake. Despite the animosity, she had to make this work.

"Rainey, so nice to see you again." Mrs. Smith clasped her hand, then patted Dorrie's head. "I hear you have some wonderful things for us to try at the festival."

Rainey nodded. "I do. I hope everyone likes them."

"Some will." The older woman's smile offered

wisdom and warmth. "And some won't, but that's the way of the world, isn't it?"

Her expression said she understood Rainey's plight and sympathized, but her smile said Rainey would be fine. And for some unknown reason, she believed her. "It is, yes."

Mrs. Smith patted her hand, still smiling. "Then we'll let God sort it out. He's much better at these things than we mere mortals."

She settled into the pew ahead, where the Cosgrove family had sat for years. Head high, she gathered up a hymnal, and her choice of seats sent a clear message that she and the pastor welcomed Rainey back into the fold. Their support blessed Rainey, but she prayed the backlash wouldn't make things hard for them.

"I love you, Mommy." Sonya slipped her hand beneath Rainey's, whispering the words she had longed to hear for three endless years. Words she thought might never come.

"Me, too." Dorrie's little fingers crept beneath Rainey's right hand. "I'm glad you came back."

Tears welled in her eyes. Her hands encased the tiny fingers. She didn't dare say a word, couldn't look down, afraid she'd fall apart in a mix of joy and regret, a swirl of emotional overload.

Just then, bright morning sun broke through the early clouds, flooding the altar with light.

As Piper handed her a tissue from her purse, Rainey breathed deep, knowing God stood near.

"Good. You dressed for the weather." Luke swept Rainey's turtleneck and fleece hoodie with a look of approval as he helped Sonya fix the buckle in the narrow middle seat. "There you go, toots."

She preened up at him. "Grandpa Charlie calls me toots, too."

"It fits you." Luke indicated Dorrie's booster seat with a glance. "It's tricky fitting three seats back here, and this is a decent-sized SUV. No wonder folks end up with minivans."

"Got it!" Rainey high-fived Dorrie after making the seat belt connection. "But I scraped myself in the process." She shook her right hand to ease the sting of the small cut as Luke rounded the car to take a look.

"Not too bad," he judged as he helped her up into the front seat. "Just needs a kiss." And with that he proceeded to kiss Rainey's hand in front of the kids.

Giggles greeted the action. "My daddy kissed your mommy!"

"I know! I saw it!"

"It was just a little kiss because she got hurt," Sonya explained in a quiet voice of reason. "Do you want me to kiss it, too, Mommy?"

"Yes, please." Rainey shot Luke a look that said he was in trouble, but he didn't care. Seeing the children's reactions reminded him of how the Campbell kids had greeted their parents' displays of affection as youngsters.

Sonya kissed the hand, then Dorrie, then Aiden, and when Rainey was finally able to turn around in the front seat, Luke sent her a sideways glance. "I'm not sorry."

"That I got hurt?"

His smile deepened. "That I kissed you. And—" he lowered his voice as he leaned closer, making the turn onto Lake Road "—I plan on doing it again. Just so you know."

She opened her mouth to argue, then eyed the children in the backseat and seemed to think better of it. For the moment, she'd stay silent.

"Rainey! I'm so glad you could make it!" Despite the brisk wind off the water, Jenny Campbell hurried outside to greet them after Luke parked the car. With no hesitation, she hugged Rainey, then turned her attention to the three five-year-olds. "Hey, you guys. Grandpa Charlie's got a project going on the front porch. Go see. After a hug, of course."

They hugged her in turn, then dashed toward the lakeside of the house. Rainey stared after them, tempted to follow. She felt safer with the kids around. Their presence meant she could bury herself in their wants and needs, and minimize adult interaction.

"You don't need them for battle armor here," Luke advised as he grabbed a box from the back of the

SUV. "My mother's been reasonably nice to my dates in the past."

Dates?

She turned to offer a quick rebuttal, but his smile said calling her his date made him happy. And seeing him happy made her long to reciprocate. But he hadn't been to church that morning. There had been lines drawn in the sand during the Sunday service, but Luke hadn't witnessed it. Maybe if he had, he'd be more cautious. About his feelings. About her.

"Come on in. That wind is biting today." Jenny took Rainey's arm and led her into a bright, spacious kitchen. "The kids are right through there, so you can see them from the front room."

"This is gorgeous," Rainey told her. The ivory kitchen balanced natural wood and paint with splashes of color from historic artifacts that hung from walls—old tools, framed magazine covers, advertisements of products long gone. The room welcomed the present while heralding the past. "You've got a great eye, Mrs. Campbell."

"Call me Jenny," Luke's mother told her as she drew Rainey forward. "Luke, get this girl something to drink, I think some of that hot cider would take the chill off."

"Rainey?"

His arched eyebrow questioned if she was okay with his mother taking charge. She smiled and nodded as Jenny led her down two stairs. "Cider would be nice."

"Rainey!" Seth hailed her from a room to the far left, and three heads poked out from the lowest level of the house. Sounds of Sunday afternoon football provided background noise. "How's it going? Glad you could make it."

"Hi, Seth."

A younger woman with milk-chocolate-colored skin and green eyes came up the four steps and moved their way. "Rainey McKinney?"

Rainey's poise nearly deserted her, but she nodded. "Yes."

"I'm Luke's sister, Cassidy."

"Oh." Rainey tried to cover her surprise and extended her hand. "Hi."

Cassidy brushed off Rainey's reaction with a grin to her mother. "Do not feel pressured to remember all of us instantly."

"All?" Rainey lifted a brow.

"There's seven of us."

"Whoa."

"God sent us four, which might have seemed like a big family to most," Jenny explained as she settled into a chair. "But I always envisioned being Mrs. Walton. The TV show, remember?"

Rainey shook her head, but Jenny just laughed.

"They had seven kids on the program. When my

body decided that four was enough, Charlie and I decided to adopt three more."

"At least she resisted the temptation to call us Jim-Bob and John-Boy," Cassidy said with a laugh.

"But only four are here today," Jenny assured her. "We're doing our annual fall birthday celebration for the ones nearby. We're thrilled that you and the girls could join us."

"Luke didn't say it was for birthdays." Rainey met Jenny's gaze. "I hope I'm not intruding."

"Nonsense. Any excuse for a party works around here. Charlie will be grilling when he's done assembling the kids' airplanes, but there are snacks down below." She nodded toward the room where hoots and hollers rose and fell on a regular basis. "And if that's too noisy, here is just fine, although we are a football-loving family."

"Everybody loves football. Don't they?"

Jenny and Cass nodded.

"Football is like apples, cider and yellow leaves," Rainey continued. "There wouldn't be fall without it."

Seth leaned around the corner of the door again. "She's a keeper, Luke."

Rainey blushed.

Luke smiled, handed her a mug of hot cider as she took a seat, then crouched low with a stern look to his mother and sister. "Do. Not. Scare. Her."

"Wouldn't think of it," Cass replied. "She's got

great hair, and this family could use some genetic help with that."

"And height," Jenny added, grinning.

"Stop analyzing her and let her relax and enjoy herself."

Rainey shooed him away. "I actually like being told I have great hair, so hush. Go watch football. I'm fine." She winked at his mother and sister.

Their answering smiles relaxed her more, Jenny pulled out a basket of knitting and curled into the wide chair opposite Rainey. Cass settled onto the sofa next to her. A big gray cat decided Cass's lap looked inviting. He landed there with an athletic leap and purred as they talked.

It felt good to be there. Normal. Relaxing. The afternoon brought to mind her mother's words about the Campbells, and how nice a family they were.

Lucia was right. The Campbell clan made you feel at home, and when they brought out cake after dinner, Rainey saw her name on the Birthday Wishes list. Surprised, emotion tightened her throat. "How did you guys know?"

"Cops know everything," Luke told her, then shrugged off the scolding look she gave him. "Zach mentioned that your birthday was the weekend of the wedding, but said you didn't want any fuss because that was Piper's time to shine. So we thought you could do a little shining of your own, here with us."

Sweet feelings overwhelmed Rainey. Surrounded

by so many Campbells, she felt as if she belonged, and Rainey hadn't felt that way in a long time.

They sang "Happy Birthday" to each person, cut slabs of cake for dessert, then Luke handed her the fleece hoodie. "Let's go for a walk so I can show you this side of the lake. Sonya? Dorrie? Aiden? You guys want to come with us?"

"Naw." Filled with cake, Aiden answered for the three of them. "Grandma said we could watch a movie in her bedroom if we promise not to eat up there."

"And we promised!" Dorrie added. "See ya."

"Just you and me," Luke mused as they headed outside, and his teasing voice said being alone with her wasn't a problem. He didn't reach for her hand, but she wanted him to, and that meant she was slipping into murky waters she'd promised to avoid. He bumped shoulders with her and pointed west. "We own nearly three hundred feet of lakefront."

"Amazing."

"Tell me about it." He nodded. "My grandfather bought this plot from old Mr. Barrett back in the fifties. He kept enough frontage for his family to access the water." Luke pointed north to a low-slung boathouse and dock. "But used the money my grandfather paid to get his farm on solid ground, and they've been secure ever since."

"It's gorgeous, Luke." The wind had quieted. The crisp autumn air hung silent and still, most of the songbirds having long since gone south. "I bet it's pretty in winter, too."

"Amazing views." He faced west and breathed deep. "You can watch storms roll in off Lake Erie. Summer and winter, you get a panoramic view of nature."

"No flooding?"

"Not here," he replied. "A bad storm can flood the southern basin near Clearwater. The creeks and the river all flow that way. They're not broad enough to handle a huge storm."

"Funny how different it is from shore to shore," Rainey mused. "Like people, really."

He accepted that. "Problems on each side, but workable if you go into it prepared."

She knew what he meant, but he was wrong. Wasn't he?

He put a light hand to the small of her back and turned her toward him. "I think I'd like to—"

Her smile said he didn't have to wait. Or ask. He lowered his lips to hers and kissed her in the chill of the autumn afternoon, beneath a grove of yellow ash. The breeze whispered through the trees, no longer stiff but sweet.

"Rainey…" Warm hands cradled her head, and the strength in his fingers fortified her. Maybe they could do this. Maybe—

"Luke?"

Cass's voice hailed them from the house. Luke's

frustrated smile said he'd like another kiss, but he grabbed Rainey's hand and moved toward the porch. "What's up?"

"Hillary's here."

Rainey sensed Luke's surprise. His expression flattened and he gave a quick nod. "Thanks, Cass."

His sister stepped aside as Luke and Rainey entered the lower level. Rainey had every intention of staying in the family room, but when Dorrie and Sonya screeched in stereo, she had no choice but to follow Luke to the living room. Wary, she stayed on the second step.

"Hillary?" Luke's voice wasn't unfriendly, but it wasn't warm, either. "What's up? You've got a puppy?"

She looked up from the floor where the three five-year-olds and his brother Jack's two boys were exclaiming over a flop-eared pup with big, flat feet. "I know how you love rescuing animals, and this guy was abandoned at Doc Schuester's. I told them I thought I knew the perfect place for him." Her wide smile in Aiden's direction said she'd included the boy in her planning, but hadn't bothered consulting the boy's father. Rainey stayed where she was, pretty sure this whole scene was about to backfire on Hillary. "He's had his first shots and he's ready for a home."

Luke frowned. "But your landlord doesn't allow dogs."

Hillary stared up at him, as if surprised he didn't

get it. From the look on Luke's face, Rainey saw that he understood the woman's intent, all right. And didn't approve.

"So where will you keep him?"

She tipped a warm gaze to Aiden once more. Luke made a show of understanding and put his hands up, palms out.

"Can't do it, but thank you for thinking of us. Our days are full as it is, and raising a puppy properly takes a lot of time and energy, neither of which we have right now. I'm sure Doc Schuester will board him until a home can be found."

"He's so cute, Dad!" Aiden piped up just then. "Aunt Hillary, are you going to keep him? Can I come visit him? Can you bring him to our house sometimes?"

Hillary splayed her hands once she stood. "I can't keep him, honey. My place is too small."

"Ours is big," Aiden noted. He turned to Luke, expectant, and that's when Hillary spotted Rainey in the stairwell.

"Oh." Her eyes narrowed. "Look who's here."

"Hillary." Luke's mother stepped forward and put a cautioning hand on the woman's arm. "We just had cake. Would you like some?"

"What I'd like is an explanation." Grief and drama shaded Hillary's gaze. Her lower lip quivered and Rainey felt as if she'd been convicted all over again. "I used to be part of all this." She indicated the

Campbell home and family gathering with a thrust of her chin. "And then *she* comes to town and everything changes. Suddenly we've got new rules and parameters for an ex-convict migrant worker. It's not enough that I lost my sister, now I've lost her son, too. Under these circumstances." She thrust a finger in Rainey's direction. "And it's just not fair."

Aiden's face crumpled.

Sonya and Dorrie stared, round-eyed, surprised by the sudden change in mood.

Tears ran down Hillary's cheeks, a silent stream of agony.

Rainey's heart went tight again. She'd promised herself to keep the girls away from all of this. And she'd warned Luke, but he hadn't listened.

The angst on Aiden's face said the little boy's joyous Sunday had ground to a halt. Luke picked him up, reassuring him in a soft, low voice. Negative emotions broadsided Rainey. She crossed the floor, took her daughters' hands and turned toward Jenny. "Can someone take me home, please?"

"I will." Charlie Campbell sent a look of displeasure to the scene behind them and grabbed Sonya's other hand. "Come on, toots, let's give you a ride in Grandpa Charlie's new truck."

"Okay." Sonya's tone said she was trying to be brave, but her face showed the struggle.

"Bye, Aiden." Dorrie hung back, clearly worried about her friend, but he didn't look their way.

Breathe, Rainey. Just breathe.

"There you go, ladies. All buckled in." Charlie climbed into the driver's seat and the look he flashed Rainey said he hated the awkwardness of the situation. He pushed in a CD and children's music flooded the cab, but neither girl sang along. Ten tedious minutes later, he pulled the truck alongside Lucia's car. Face grim, he helped release Dorrie from the second seat, then turned to Rainey. "I just want to say I'm sorry."

She shooed the girls toward the house once they said their goodbyes, and turned to Luke's dad, striving for a calm she didn't feel. "I'm sorry, too. Because I knew better. Please thank Mrs. Campbell for me. I'm afraid I forgot to do that before we left."

Charlie looked as if he wanted to say more, but what was there to say? Once an albatross, always an albatross. She gave him a little wave and went into the house, hoping no one would be there to see her face, read her feelings. She wanted a little time to pray.

She shut her phone off, read the girls a couple stories, turned on their favorite princess movie and started baking cookies for next week's wedding. By the time the family came back from Zach's place next door, trays of chocolate chip cookies filled every available counter space in the kitchen, and both tables. Plastic freezer tubs were set up, ready to fill.

Lucia stared at her, hard.

Rainey pretended not to notice.

Piper studied the girls, then Rainey, and moved close. "Tell me who hurt you and I'll deck them."

"Me," Rainey replied. She faced her mom and sister firmly and met their combined looks of concern. "Trying too much, too soon, and thinking everyone else is on board. My mistake."

"It is not right to treat one poorly, ever," Lucia insisted in a tight whisper, but Rainey held up a hand to stop her.

"Sin has shrapnel." She raised her shoulders, then dropped them. "My actions hurt others. And yes, it was years ago, but some scars go deep. Some of that collateral damage is coming back to haunt me."

"And if they never heal? How is that your fault?"

Rainey considered Piper's words and shrugged. "Coming back home has reopened old wounds. People are taking sides, and I hate that, but I'm here to stay. Having said that…" She aimed a look at the precious little girls cuddled in a brightly striped afghan on the living room sofa with two sleeping kittens tucked into their laps. "I won't continue to put them in the line of fire, and that means I'll stay closer to home until things get better."

"They will." Lucia grabbed her into a hug, and for the first time, Rainey felt the tears she'd held at bay threaten. Her mother's love meant a great deal after all she'd done to hurt this woman. "God is greater than all things human. He alone lights our path and charts our way. In Him all good things come."

Rainey had clung to that in Illinois. She'd do the same now. "I love you, Mama. And you." She sent Piper a watery smile over her stout mother's shoulder. "And now, ladies." She stepped back, swiped her apron hem across her eyes and faced them. "We have a wedding next weekend and cookies to freeze. Let's get busy."

The squad commander gave Luke's banged-up hand a cryptic look the next afternoon. "How does the other guy look?"

"It was a wall, thanks. No significant damage."

"That's a well-built wall," the officer noted. "Wanna talk about it?"

"No."

"Woman?"

"No. Well. Partly. But she didn't cause this."

The commander studied him, and Luke knew why. He looked bad. Tired. Surly. He'd taken Hillary's angst and abuse, and then his family had dumped their opinions on him, as well.

Jack made it clear that Luke should have taken charge long ago. If he had, that scene with Hillary never would have taken place.

Cass said Rainey had looked brokenhearted when Hillary's barrage began. Luke had been too busy protecting Aiden to notice.

And the girls, those little girls, having someone disparage their mother in their presence. What effect would that have on them?

Aiden was mad at him for refusing the puppy, his mother didn't look any too pleased with him or Hillary, and his father refused to talk about Rainey's reaction on the drive home, leaving Luke in the dark.

His calls to her cell phone went straight to voice mail. And he wasn't about to call the house phone and have Lucia ream him out. He'd stop by and let Rainey's mother have a piece of him in person, although that idea didn't thrill him.

Luke faced the commander as he donned his deputy's hat. "Family stuff. I took a look in a mirror yesterday and the image I saw wasn't pretty."

The man accepted that. "You're okay to work?"

"Yes. More mad at myself than anyone, but I'll work it out."

"Time helps." The commander paused, then added, "And prayer. I can't imagine doing this job and not being tight with God."

His words niggled Luke. The squad commander was a hard man, schooled in the streets and good at his job. Prayerful? Luke wouldn't have guessed it.

"Campbell, you've been solid for years. If this messes with your head too much, call me. Don't let a momentary glitch stain years of hard work and good judgment."

Wise words. Luke nodded. "Will do."

He longed to go see Rainey, deal with this face-to-face, but as he headed that way on his lunch break, a hint of reason made him pause.

Time. Give her time.

He scoffed at the internal warning, but it came again. *Time...*

He glared at his watch as common sense prevailed. Once he got there, he'd barely have time to approach the subject of yesterday, apologize and deal with the backlash. And then he'd have to leave to get back to work, with things in an upheaval.

Not smart.

But what could he do? How could he ease this? She'd predicted his reaction—that if someone attacked her, he'd protect Aiden. He'd done exactly that, and left her to take Hillary's shots alone.

He was ashamed of himself. Worse, he'd disgusted his family, and that wake-up call dealt a hard blow. They'd been right all this time. He'd shrugged off their concerns and advice until it blew up in his mother's living room.

He'd hurt Aiden, the girls and Rainey, and that meant he had a lot of fixing to do. But how?

Piper's wedding was Saturday. Five days away. The whole family had lists to take care of, wedding assignments they'd worked out to help the day run smoothly.

Like it or not, he needed to wait. He'd messed up, but right now Rainey and her family had days of preparation ahead. Maybe he could ease that, maybe not. But he had no right stirring things up so close to Piper's wedding.

A plan formed in his head. It started small, but as pieces fell into place, he saw a chance to help. A little generosity was the least he could do.

Luke had stopped calling.

He didn't send flowers or chocolates or any of the other typical things guys did when they were in trouble. All she had was a three-sentence note of apology she'd received late Monday: "Rainey, I'm sorry for what happened yesterday. I didn't foresee anything like that. Please forgive me. Luke."

You called it. You knew what would happen. Why were you surprised and hurt when it did?

Because she'd let herself dream. Her fault, entirely. She listened to the rainy forecast for Saturday's festivities and sighed inside. Bake cookies or clean the barn?

The barn won out, because their guests couldn't be left standing in the rain. The freshly painted barn was their alternative wedding site, and while not used for animals, it wasn't exactly company-ready inside. But with rain predicted, she needed to get the place in shape. Marly and Noreen could handle the store for the day. Piper and Marty were thick into harvesting, and despite the wedding, Piper had a job to do on the farm.

Once the girls were on the school bus, Rainey changed into old sweats and headed for the barn.

A truck pulled into the driveway. It wound its way slowly toward her and rolled to a stop not far from the house and dairy store. Two sturdy men climbed out of the cab. The driver approached her and handed her an invoice. "Good morning, ma'am. Are you Miss McKinney?"

"Yes." Rainey scanned the paper and frowned. "I don't understand."

"The wedding tent, miss." The driver waited patiently, but Rainey knew he must be wondering why she hesitated. "Where would you like it?"

"I'd love it right there," she told him, pointing to the broad patch of grass between the dairy store and the house. "But we didn't order a tent." Piper had seen the cost of tent rental and nixed that idea. Even with Marty's help, her frugal side had prevailed.

"Then that's where we'll put it," the man said. He tipped his hat, but Rainey darted around front to stop him.

"But we didn't pay for a tent," she tried to explain.

The man smiled as if money was no big deal. "All paid for, ma'am. No charge to you."

All paid for?

Rainey's to-do list loosened up with the thought of not having to attack the barn. The men hauled out the tent on a long, wheeled dolly, positioned it in place and began unrolling the huge white canvas shelter.

Marty, she decided. Marty must have seen the sense of providing a roof for his son's wedding and ordered the tent despite Piper's financial misgivings. Rainey called him on his cell phone.

"Marty, the tent's here and I wanted to thank you," she exclaimed when he answered. The rumble of the combine competed with his voice, but Rainey heard the last part loud and clear.

"I didn't order a tent, Rainey."

He didn't? "Zach, then?"

"I doubt it. I think he figured if Piper wanted a tent, she'd have okayed it."

True enough. Rainey watched the men, torn. Should she make them wait? The driver had said it was paid in full. So why stop them? "All right. But when your partner gets home and sees this beautiful wedding tent in the yard, she's going to ask some questions, and I have no answers."

"Blame those elves you were telling the girls about the other night," Marty suggested, laughing.

"I'll see you later, Marty."

"Will do."

She watched the men another moment, then realized she was wasting time. Whoever had sent the heavy-duty tent would be blessed by her prayers of thanksgiving and lots of cookies at the wedding feast. She went back into the house, pointed out the front-yard activity to her mother and turned on the double ovens, thrilled that baking cookies took precedence over sweeping spiderwebs.

Chapter Ten

"Do you have a sitter for Piper's wedding tomorrow?" Jenny asked Luke Friday night.

He hedged. "Kim and Jack said they'd take Aiden to the zoo with them if I needed someone."

"If?" Jenny tugged on her jacket and gathered her knitting bag. "It's your friend's wedding. You're invited. Of course you're going."

Luke had been struggling with that question since Sunday. "I'm not sure my presence will be all that welcome."

"Because of Hillary's performance last weekend," Jenny noted. "Have you talked to Rainey? Apologized?"

"No, and before you ream me out, it's because I know how busy they are this week. I don't want to add any more drama to the wedding preparations while she's also working and taking care of the girls. She told me she's spending this week focusing on the wedding and Piper. In that order. But I did send a note. And a tent. With tables and chairs."

Jenny made a face. "You what?"

"You think it was dumb?" Luke scowled and rubbed the nape of his neck. "I saw the forecast and knew they didn't want to spend extra money on a wedding tent, but Rainey said she'd use her day off cleaning the barn for the wedding if we expected rain. I figured a tent would buy her some time. Was that a stupid idea?"

His mother's smile assured him it wasn't. "You did good. Does she know it was from you?"

He shook his head quickly. "I wasn't looking for thanks. I just wanted to make her life easier."

Jenny reached up and hugged him. "The gift of time is the best present ever. And don't you forget that. I've got to run, but I'll see you tomorrow. At the wedding."

Undecided, he shrugged. "We'll see."

"Children learn what they live," she reminded him as she walked to the door. "You've got that poem on the wall of Aiden's room. Might be a good time to reread it."

Luke knew she was right. He needed to take charge of his own life if he expected his son to do the same. And Piper had been his friend for several years. She'd been a huge support after Martha's death. His mother's expression said he'd be wrong to miss this wedding.

He called Jack, firmed up plans for Aiden, then circled the barns before he called it a night. Spirit nickered, then padded across the soft dirt, looking for a nose rub. Luke gave the horse some well-deserved attention and a promise. "We'll take a ride soon. Life's been busy, old man."

The horse leaned into his touch. The tired movement told Luke that Spirit didn't care all that much about riding. He just wanted attention now and again. Rubbing the horse's head and neck calmed them both.

Luke decided he would go to the wedding. If things seemed uncomfortable for Rainey, he'd duck out of the reception. But the idea of seeing Rainey in a bridesmaid dress?

That image alone was enough to put a smile on his face.

Rainey reexamined her checklist on Friday afternoon. So far, so good. Lucia came through the kitchen door with a clutch of mail and handed her an official-looking envelope.

The return address made Rainey cringe. "A letter from school. I'm afraid to open it."

Lucia dismissed her concern. "The girls are doing much better. I see it in the papers they bring home, their little projects. You are doing well, Larraina."

"We'll see." Rainey slit the envelope with a butter knife, opened the sheet inside, then read aloud,

"'Dear Ms. McKinney, it is my pleasure to inform you that both Dorrie and Sonya are adjusting well. The problems we discussed are abating and both teachers report above-grade-level assessments in reading and mathematics. Behavioral concerns have been minimized. Whatever you're doing, keep it up. Your girls are a delight. Frank O'Mara, Principal, Kirkwood Lake Elementary School.'"

"I am correct once more, it seems." Lucia smiled broadly as she hugged Rainey from behind. "I hope young Aiden has received a similar good report."

Rainey hoped so, too, but she hadn't heard from Luke since she'd received his note. She thought wedding prep would leave her too busy to care. It didn't, but she'd pushed thoughts of Sunday's drama to the back of her mind. This week was about Piper and Zach. Come Sunday she could refocus on the festival and the upcoming holidays. And maybe think about how much she missed Luke.

"The tables and chairs are set up." Berto walked into the kitchen and motioned to her sheet. "I do not remember them on our list."

"They weren't. We have picnic tables for guests," Rainey replied. "That's why we sanded and painted them."

"Well, there is seating for over a hundred out there." Her uncle waved to the yard. "And nice tables and chairs. No one will have to climb into a seat in their pretty dresses now."

First the tent. Now tables and chairs.

Rainey and Lucia walked outside. The day had started bright, but increasing clouds said rain was imminent. Even so, the guests would be warm and dry inside the large tent. Rainey, Marly and Noreen had decorated the interior with fall-colored silk flowers and ribbons. They'd crafted candle-filled Mason jars of varying heights for simple, vintage centerpieces. Tomorrow they'd arrange small gourds and pumpkins around the jars, the clutch of fall colors a contrast to the burlap tablecloth background. With the dairy store closed for the day, Marly and Noreen were free to oversee the guests' comfort.

"This looks wonderful. And when I find out who ordered this setup—" she fingered the tent's thick canvas "—I'm going to kiss him. Or her." She looked at her mother, but Lucia stepped back.

"Not me. My bank account empties each week. But I am glad, as well. This looks as a wedding should look."

It did.

Piper was surprised but pleased. She'd scolded Zach and Marty for not obeying her wishes.

They denied knowledge of the tent and the seating.

She looked dubious, but it didn't matter. Tomorrow they'd have room to sit, eat, dance and gather around the happy couple.

Save a dance for me....

Rainey pushed the thought of Luke's request aside. She wouldn't think of him this weekend. Come Monday, she'd re-strategize her feelings. But right now, she had a wedding to help host. Making Piper's day perfect was more important than anything.

Gorgeous.

Luke had taken a spot near the edge of the dock, out of the press of folks surrounding the gazebo. Forecasters had predicted rain by noon, the time of the wedding. He hoped they could get everyone up the hill to the warm, waiting tent before the heavens opened up.

And then Rainey stepped into view with her daughters, and his brain was wiped clean.

The girls were twin bursts of color and energy in bright pink gowns with gathered, tucked skirts that fell to the floor—two miniature princesses, precious and sweet.

Rainey's deep purple gown was made of some kind of thin, gauzy fabric that swirled with her every move. It was fitted on top. Below the waistline, the skirt flared and whispered as she monitored the girls.

Luke stayed in the background, out of her line of vision, but when she scanned the crowd, he wondered why.

Was she looking for him?

The music started. Luke's vantage point gave him a clear view, and as Piper followed Sonya, Dorrie and Rainey into the vintage gazebo, the wedding party formed a picturesque image of new beginnings.

Luke longed for a similar chance. A chance to begin anew. He didn't deserve it; he knew that. But that didn't stop him from wanting to take that step. With Rainey.

Rainey spotted Luke at the far end of the tent as the bride and groom shared their first dance as husband and wife. He raised a glass of punch and dipped his chin, a silent hello.

She'd looked for him at the ceremony, but the press of people around the gazebo kept him hidden from sight. Seeing him now, in a fitted, dark blue suit, made her wish things were different.

She helped Piper adjust her veil for the cake-cutting, then gathered food for the bride and groom's dinner. She laughed when the bridal bouquet landed in the arms of Mrs. Thurgood, a widow from the village who sold her crocheted afghans in local venues.

Rainey had pledged her time and service to Piper and Zach, and despite the rain showers, the day was heartfelt and beautiful. A day to thank God for second chances and new beginnings.

A hand touched her back. She didn't have to turn

to know who it was, but she turned anyway, hoping she could hide her feelings.

"I believe I requested a dance?" Luke's hand gently pulled her to the small dance floor at the front of the tent. "And the DJ is playing our song."

"We don't have a song."

"We do now."

Her heart melted as the opening chord to Lonestar's "Amazed" came through the speakers, but she hardened it again when she thought of last Sunday's spectacle. Whatever Luke's issues were, her past and his present didn't mix. She couldn't forget that, and her girls didn't need any more drama in their lives. And that thought reminded her of yesterday's letter. "I got a very nice letter from Mr. O'Mara."

She pulled back to glance at Luke's face, but he drew her close again. The movement of his head against her hair confirmed he'd gotten a letter also. "Mine said my kid was making great strides and that Miss Patterson is pleased with his turnaround in behavior. Which, of course—" this time Luke pulled back and met her gaze "—I owe to you."

"To us," Rainey corrected.

He laughed softly. "Only because I started swallowing my pride and taking advice. Anyway, he's doing better, still shy, but participating. And answering questions. That's a big step forward for Aiden."

"Luke, I—"

"Let's not talk about Sunday now. Please."

He'd read her mind, but it wasn't hard to do. Sunday's events had created a chasm between them, with no bridge in sight. "We can't ignore it," she told him.

His sigh said he agreed.

"But it can wait, I suppose."

He smiled against her hair. "Thank you."

The song drew to a sweet conclusion. Rainey didn't want the music to end. Luke's expression mirrored her thoughts. But then Sonya and Dorrie clapped their hands and raced to her side. "Mommy! They're playing the 'Hokey Pokey' and we know it!"

"Then let's dance." Rainey grabbed Sonya's hand. Luke gripped Dorrie's. As people filled in the circle for the kid-friendly dance, Luke and Rainey ended up on opposite sides. The sight of him dancing with Dorrie, the way her daughter's bright smile met his, brought Rainey's buried dreams back into the light.

He cared about her girls. He cared about her. But emotions weren't always reflected in actions. Rainey knew that. Right now, seeing Luke with Dorrie, she wondered if her hopes and dreams might really be possible.

As the reception wound down, a local farmer approached Rainey about carrying his family's scented, goat-milk soaps in the store. "I'd love to talk to you more about it later," she answered, then redirected her attention to the girls. "But I've got to get these two to bed. It's been a long day."

"I'll help." Luke stepped up from behind and picked up Dorrie. "Come on, snugglebun, let's get you inside. The temperature's taking a nosedive out here."

"I want to wear my bunny jammies," Dorrie told him, but a yawn distorted the last words. "I love my bunny jammies."

"Are they clean?" Luke knew that busy single parents didn't always have total command of laundry.

Rainey's soft smile said she understood. "Clean enough," she told him. They took the girls inside. Lucia was working with a small crew of women in the kitchen. A pot of fresh coffee and a plate of Rainey's cookies added to the down-home feeling.

They took the back stairs to the girls' bedroom. In five minutes they had the two changed, teeth brushed and tucked into twin beds pushed side by side.

"They don't like being separated, do they?" Luke whispered as their eyes drifted shut.

"No. But they're getting better about it," Rainey replied as she walked him downstairs. She excused herself for a moment, went back upstairs, then returned a few minutes later in jeans, a turtleneck and a sweatshirt. "Round two—cleanup."

"I'll help."

"You're all dressed up," she scolded.

"Then I'll help carefully."

The outside crew had stacked the cleared tables and a good share of the chairs onto dollies. The rain had moved on, but the cold, wet ground around the tent reminded Luke that change had come. Fall was a short season near Lake Erie, and November snow wasn't uncommon.

Once the last of the guests said their goodbyes, Lucia called a halt to cleanup. "The little we have left can be handled after church tomorrow," she announced. "It is time to rest."

Within minutes, Luke and Rainey were alone in the farmhouse kitchen. She opened the fridge, pulled out a bottle, poured the contents into two cups and heated them in the microwave. Once it was done, she handed one to Luke and led the way into the living room, where a small fire glowed in the soapstone stove.

She sipped lightly and indicated Luke's mug with a glance. "Tell me what you think."

He sank into the chair opposite hers, made a show of eyeing the cup with suspicion, then sniffed, sipped and smiled. "That's delicious. Hot cinnamon milk?"

"Soothing and warming. Mama used to make this for me when I was little. Cinnamon settles the stomach, she says."

"The scent alone should sell it." He sat back, knowing they needed to discuss things other than milk. "Rainey, I—"

"Luke—"

They spoke in unison, then paused. Luke gave way. "Ladies first."

Rainey's bittersweet smile made him wish he could backtrack to last Sunday and fix things, but he couldn't. Maybe she'd allow him to move forward. Maybe not.

"I love that the kids' behavior is improving," she began. "I think your idea is working brilliantly and it shows in so many ways. Sonya and Aiden are more verbal, they're laughing more and accepting changes. That's a huge step forward."

"You're telling me the positives to get me ready before you hit me with the negatives," he assumed. Her guilty look said he was right. "I know what you mean, Rain. And I know how badly I messed up last Sunday." He leaned forward, hands clasped. "And it's not my first mess-up, but you've helped me see that my behavior was influencing Aiden's. We were enabling each other."

"You had help."

She meant Hillary, and obviously wondered how two adults could possibly be so very wrong about one little kid. Which meant he needed to tell her the truth. "Losing Martha was hard."

Rainey nodded. Her look of sympathy said she couldn't imagine the grief of burying a loved one so young.

"But having Aiden come through it alive made

me so grateful that I went a little crazy, trying to keep him safe. Happy. Well-adjusted. And in doing that, I messed him up."

"Aiden came through *what* alive?" Her knitted brow said she had no idea what he was talking about. A part of Luke wished Piper had filled her in, but Piper respected his privacy.

"My wife killed herself, Rainey."

His unexpected words hit Rainey hard. But the follow-up only made it worse.

"Martha dealt with ongoing depression after Aiden's birth. I thought it was getting better. Now I know she was pretending, but back then I hoped and prayed we could conquer her feelings. Get on with our lives. We were so happy together, and all I wanted was to reclaim that joy." He sat quietly for a moment, eyes down, hands clasped, then sighed. "One day she asked me to take Aiden to day care. I was running late and said no."

His grim look made Rainey's heart ache.

"She drove into the hills. It was late fall, and the days weren't too bad, but the nights were bitter cold. She disappeared, and we spent two days hunting for her, for Aiden, for the car. For forty-eight hours I had no idea where she'd gone. What had happened. There was no note, no indication of what she wanted to do, just that request to take Aiden to day care. Which I'd refused."

Long seconds ticked by.

Rainey sat silent, praying for him. She couldn't imagine his pain then, but she saw the pain now. Pain and guilt, a wretched combination.

"They found the car on Sunday afternoon, just before dark. Martha had gone into the lake and left Aiden inside the car. The doors were locked. He must have wriggled out of his seat because the straps were still locked in place. He hadn't had a diaper change or food for two days, but he'd found a half-filled water bottle in a cup holder and drank that."

The thought of that little boy, desperate and alone for two days...

Rainey's heart broke.

This was why Luke coddled the child. This was why he'd bent over backward to make Aiden's world safe and serene. He'd tried to soften his son's trauma by going overboard the other way. "Luke, I'm so sorry. So very sorry."

"I know." He stared at the floor for a moment, then sighed. "I didn't mean to dump all this on you, but I don't want you thinking I'm overprotective for no good reason."

She nodded, empathetic. "And now?"

"Now I need to back off. You've showed me that, and I can see that it's working. But last Sunday, when Hillary took those shots at you, when she put him in the middle with the puppy, all I could see was that I needed to protect him. And I did. But I left you in the cold, and that was wrong."

He raised his gaze to Rainey's and in his eyes she saw a hint of hope. "I want another chance," he told her. "I want you to give me a chance to prove myself to you. I can't promise I won't mess up, but I'll try not to. And that should count for something, Rain."

His confession blindsided her, but cleared up some confusion, as well. Luke was a cop for good reason. He was a protector. The shock at not being able to help his wife and protect his child had broadsided *him*. And refusing to take Aiden to day care that day?

That innocent choice compounded his guilt.

Rainey stood. So did Luke.

She reached for his hands, and his gentle grasp made her heart sigh. "It counts for a lot, Luke. I've made serious mistakes in my life, but that's in the past, and I'm determined to embrace the present and make a good future for my daughters. But like you, I have to be careful. I can't risk messing them up any more than I already have. And my past is still tripping up my present."

He started to contradict her, but she silenced him with a shake of her head. "I own my past, but I'm claiming my future. So, yes."

His quick smile said he liked the sound of that word.

"Yes, I'd like to see where *this* goes. You and

me." She gripped his fingers tighter. "Because I care about you, Luke. Way more than I should."

He stepped closer and drew her into a warm hug. The shelter of his arms said she'd come home at last, and Rainey relished the feeling.

"I watched that wedding," he whispered, "and all I could think of was how happy Piper and Zach are now. How she went through so much with her family, but it's come out all right. I want that, Rain. I want a second chance." He hugged her tighter, his cheek against her hair, his voice husky with emotion. "I didn't think I deserved it, but watching them, seeing you and the girls with them... I knew I wanted a chance at that happiness. I started to think that maybe I wasn't so undeserving after all."

"Guilt makes a poor master." Rainey laid her head against his shoulder. The steady beat of his strong heart soothed her fears and concerns. "Jesus was abandoned by so many of His friends at His darkest hour. And still He came back to them, blessing them with the Holy Spirit. That's the kind of love God wants for us. Things happen, but He wants us to move on. Be free of guilt. He wants His children happy."

"My mother has told me that same thing." Luke leaned down and caught Rainey's lips in a gentle kiss. "I have trouble believing it, but it gives her strength."

"He who forgives little is loved little," Rainey

quoted softly. "But he who has been forgiven the most, loves the most." She looked up at the clock and pulled back. "You must go. I have to be up with the girls in time to help with chores and get them to church. And I'm working at the store tomorrow, so my day is spoken for."

"Me, too. I'll call you. Maybe we can get together this week."

She pointed to the calendar on the wall. "Not a chance. I have to get my holiday displays done, put together a slew of gift baskets, make my cakes and bottle the milks I need to transport, plus maintain some level of normalcy for the girls."

"Then we'll have two days together at the festival." His expression said he hated to wait, but Rainey knew her limits. Making this festival successful was important to her. God had led her back here to make amends, not make things worse. And that's what she was going to do.

"Yes. Between now and then, I'm swamped."

"I can help."

She shook her head. "You can't, not really, unless you take the girls for a few hours here and there. That would be a huge help."

"And a delight." Luke grinned, swept a kiss across her mouth and grazed her cheek with his hand. "You are so very beautiful, Rain."

"It was a great dress, wasn't it?" She smiled,

pleased that he'd noticed. But then he moved closer and pressed a gentle kiss to her cheek, her ear.

"Not the dress," he whispered. "The woman wearing the dress. You're just as beautiful right now. And if hearing that makes you blush, then get ready to blush often, because I love telling you that."

She dropped her chin, embarrassed, but he smiled, kissed her cheek one last time and backed away. "I'll take the girls on Tuesday after school. And then bring them here after supper, okay?"

"Okay." Rainey wanted to sound strong, matter-of-fact, but her voice betrayed her emotions.

He winked, turned and jogged down the steps and across the yard in his well-fitted suit. At the bottom he turned. "So. You liked the tent? And the tables and chairs?"

He'd sent them to save her time. To make things easier for her. Her heart stretched wider and she leaned against the porch post, smiling. "Yes, thank you. You shouldn't have spent all that money, but they made my life much easier this week."

"That's all I wanted." He ducked into the car and offered a silent salute with his hand.

As she watched him drive away, her thoughts went back to what he'd told her about his wife. Her death. Aiden.

Luke's honesty shed a new light on him. She saw his earnest attempts to change things to help his son, and she applauded his goals. But two people burdened by so much baggage might not be a good combination, and Rainey had no intention of wading into uncharted waters. Part of her loved Luke's attention.

But her precious girls came first, no matter what. Prayer and time would remain her two best friends, and she had no trouble using both to avoid more mistakes.

Chapter Eleven

"I'm kidnapping you and the girls as promised."
Luke strode into the dairy store at three o'clock on
Tuesday afternoon and reached for her hand. "The
twins are already buckled in the car. Come on."

"I can't." She planted her feet and heard Marly
laugh behind her. "You're supposed to take them,
not me. We're busy."

"Your mother is coming over to cover. She knows
you need a break. So do I. It's been a crazy couple
of weeks for you, with more to come." He steered
Rainey toward the door, grabbed her jacket from a
hook and waved to Marly, then Lucia as they met
in the doorway. "See you later, ladies."

"Luke, I—"

He turned, stopped and simply held her gaze.

"Oh. Well. When you look at me like that…" she
grumbled as she followed him to the SUV.

"Like?"

"All puppy-dog cute and expectant. It's almost irresistible."

"I'll make note of that." He pulled into his mother's drive about fifteen minutes later and tooted the horn.

Jenny and Aiden came out the side door, smiling.

The girls barreled out of the car and charged toward the house. As Rainey started to release her seat belt, Luke put out a restraining hand. "We're not staying."

"What do you mean?"

He grinned, waved to the kids and laughed at Rainey's confused expression as he backed onto the road. "You and I are going horseback riding."

The thought of riding made her smile. Luke's timing didn't. "I should be making signs for the booth tonight. Putting together gift basket arrangements. Tying Indian corn into bunches for decorations."

"Except the festival takes us right into holiday time," he reminded her as he pulled into his driveway. "So relaxing on one of the few nice days we might enjoy until next spring isn't exactly a crime. I promised Spirit and Star we'd take them out." He got out of the car, came around and reached for her hand, then led her to the barn. "We've only got about ninety minutes of daylight, so let's not waste it arguing, okay? Let's just ride."

He'd saddled the horses before coming to pick her up. Star was antsy, but Spirit stood waiting, patient and strong. "You take Spirit," Luke said. "Star gets twitchy when she's been corralled too long."

The big, dark horse breathed deep as Rainey drew near, then puffed out a long breath, a sigh of excitement.

"See that?" Luke smiled as he gave her a leg up. "He's happy to be hitting the trails with you."

Spirit *was* happy. Rainey sensed it in the quiver of his withers, the angle of his head, the way he tipped an ear toward her, waiting for her command. "Okay, Spirit. Let's take a walk, shall we?"

Luke led the way out of the paddock and across the back field. His house sat midway up a sloping hill overlooking Kirkwood Lake. A creek curled downhill, not too deep right now, but a true gully washer during spring runoff. They rode together through the woods and down the hill, not pushing the horses. When they reached a broad, bright meadow, Luke gave Star her head and let her run.

Spirit followed suit, but didn't race. He kept his pace measured and smooth, and when Star finally paused, panting, Spirit kept on, a true distance runner. When Luke gave a hand signal, Rainey slowed the aged horse into a cool-down walk.

"This way." Luke waved toward the drop-off south of them. "There's a great view over here."

As they approached the edge, Rainey caught her breath. "Oh, Luke. This is gorgeous."

The ground beneath them ended in a steep drop to

the creek far below. Beyond the thin curve of water, a finger of land stretched into the lake. The village of Warrentown nestled on the narrow peninsula, making a picture-postcard scene with its old homes, new cottages, mature trees and spired churches.

"Pretty from up here, isn't it?" he asked.

"Not pretty." He'd brought Star alongside Spirit and Rainey turned to face him. "Stunning. It's like a Currier and Ives print."

"I love it," he told her. His expression turned more contemplative as he indicated his acreage with a shrug of one shoulder. "I bought this after Martha died. I needed a new beginning. I couldn't face our old house, and Aiden was young enough that he doesn't recall the other place. This has been home to him for as long as he can remember."

"It's beautiful, Luke. A perfect place to raise your son."

His smile deepened. "Of course, we've got lots of room here."

She knew what he was hinting at. That there was plenty of room here for her and the girls. But she wanted to take things slow. Why wouldn't her heart obey her head?

"You do," she answered, then turned Spirit to start the uphill climb, changing the subject at the same time. "It's getting late and I don't want Spirit to stumble in the shadows. Not at his age."

"I know." Luke's voice revealed his true affection

for the horse. "He's rallied through good times and bad, but his days are growing short. I dread saying goodbye to him." Luke hesitated, then added, "It's probably not good for me to get so attached, but in some cases, like Spirit's, I do."

"Loving your animals isn't a bad thing," Rainey scolded lightly. "How old is he?"

"Twenty-seven last month."

She made a sound of sympathy that Luke acknowledged with a nod. "I try to prepare myself, but I'm never really successful. Does that make me a sap?"

"It makes you a wonderful man with a big heart," she told him. "It's also what makes you a good cop, Luke. Strength and empathy. The sheriff's department is blessed to have you."

"Thank you." He smiled at her, matched Star's pace to Spirit's and ducked beneath a low branch. "We'll get these guys put up, then have supper at my mother's. She made a pot of stew that the kids might not like, but we will. And just in case they're not big fans, she's got Dad making hot dogs on the griddle."

"Our backup plan most days," laughed Rainey.

Once they finished tending the horses, she paused and placed a hand on his arm.

He glanced down, and the easy look of affection in those blue eyes called to her.

"Thank you for this." She settled her gaze on the contented pair of horses. "I didn't know I needed this, but you did, so thank you." She stretched up on tiptoe and kissed his cheek. "Thank you so much."

His smile called her closer, and she couldn't refuse a sweet, shared moment beneath the gold-leafed maple. His kiss said he liked sharing time with her, alone. Talking. Laughing. Courting.

She sighed and pulled back. "Supper."

He agreed with reluctance. "All right. But I'm glad you enjoyed the ride. Spirit did, too."

She'd felt the horse's joy as they'd started out, but she'd sensed his tiredness at the end, too. "It was the perfect length for him at this stage. Just enough."

"Funny, when I think about time with you, the word *enough* never enters into the picture, Rain." They climbed into his SUV and he started the engine, then turned to her. "And I love feeling that way. So if you share those feelings, blink once. If not, just pretend I didn't say anything, okay?"

She smiled and gave one long, slow blink.

He grinned, put the vehicle in gear and headed back up the road. "I was hoping you'd say that."

Luke looked over a checklist the following night. "Booth is made."

"Check."

"Cinnamon milk is bottled."

"Yes."

"Cakes and Christmas gift baskets are made for sampling and display."

"Yes."

"You're worried about this weekend."

Rainey scowled as she drizzled milk syrup on the last cake. "Let's not mention it, okay?"

"Okay. But a wise woman told me that warm cinnamon milk is soothing. You might want to try some."

She made a face at him, then straightened when a knock sounded at the door.

"I will answer." Lucia made her way past three tired kids in the living room. She opened the door, then waved the person in. "Come in, Lacey. How are you? How is your father doing?"

Lacey Barrett unwound her scarf and shook her head. "Not well, I'm afraid. Aunt Ellen is there right now, so I wanted to get over here and talk to Rainey. Mostly because Dad insisted."

"Of course." Rainey motioned to a chair at the table. "Let me finish this cake and I'm all yours."

"Here, Lacey, sit down." Luke pulled the chair out and then nodded toward the front room. "I'm going to grab Aiden and head home, Rainey. You're okay with our setup plans for tomorrow?"

"Where you and Marty do all the work while I get food ready?" She smiled. "I'm totally in favor of that idea."

"Good."

"Good." Lucia added her agreement, then offered Lacey coffee.

"No, not now, I'd never sleep, but thank you, Lucia. What I'd like to do is talk to Rainey about carrying our apple products at your store, and we'd reciprocate by offering a cooler of your dairy products on our side of the lake. With the weather turning and the holidays coming, it makes sense to diversify what we offer our customers. And we all know people are more reluctant to drive distances in the winter."

"Great idea, Lacey," Luke called out from the front room.

"I'd love that," Rainey replied. But she couldn't let Lacey come into this without being honest. "Our business is down, though. Since I took over."

She didn't wait for her reply, but moved across the kitchen, kissed Aiden goodbye and shared a smile with Luke, returning to the table once the two of them had left. "I don't want to put you in an awkward position," she explained. "Your family has been good to so many in this community."

"Well, this isn't about being good," Lacey replied, though Rainey was pretty sure the woman's giving nature was what had spawned the current offer. "It's about good business and winter approaching. I see this as a smart business arrangement."

"Mutually beneficial," Rainey supplied, and Lacey laughed.

"Yes. Perfect. Anyway, we're at one of those crossroads in life. With Dad in hospice care, I have to start making decisions that will keep our fruit farm afloat for the next generation. And I think you're in a similar circumstance. When I heard you were carrying Testy's smoked meats, I realized we could do the same kind of thing without affecting each other's sales."

She was right. Not too many people enjoyed the slow, meandering drive around the lake in the winter. Rainey put out her hand as Lacey stood. "I think this is a great idea, Lacey. Mama? Do you agree?"

"I do. And we'll let Piper and Marty know what we're doing. Even in the summer, people love being *on* the lake, but they do not love driving *around* it."

Lacey nodded. "You're right."

Lucia wrapped up a loaf of bread, then a large hunk of the fresh cake. "Keep this in the refrigerator, and put whipped cream on top when you're ready for dessert. It is so good, your family will love it. And take with you our prayers for your father and the whole family," Lucia added. She reached out and hugged the younger woman. "*Vaya con Dios*, Lacey."

"Thank you, Lucia." Gratitude deepened Lacey's tone. "We're planning on being at the festival, unless Dad's situation changes. He wouldn't hear of canceling the booth for something as simple as cancer." Her expression said that the tough old farmer who had raised her was in charge to the end, and no one was about to thwart his wishes. "My older brother has come back to town. To stay."

"I am surprised," Lucia admitted.

"Here's a bigger surprise," Lacey told her. "He's taking over as manager of Kirkwood Lodge again."

"Now that it sputters in red ink." Lucia's expression turned dour. "Perhaps this is a good wake-up call for many, but for now, it is just nice to have Greg here to help with your father. And for us to do business with Barrett's Orchards."

"I agree."

Rainey reached out a hand to Lacey and was surprised when Lacey offered her a hug instead. "We women need to stick together. It's good to have you home, Rainey. And seeing Luke here when I walked in?" Lacey grinned as she pulled open the door. "Pretty sweet. We'd all like to see him happy."

"Well, I—"

Lacey waved off any reply she tried to make. "I'll keep it to myself, but I want you to know it made my day, seeing him looking so content. God bless you, Rainey."

Lacey's open nature, and her offer of shelf space at their busy farm store, lifted Rainey's spirits. The latter might mean a push for their dairy. It could also indicate that her homecoming might be starting to right itself, one step at a time.

"Where was this gorgeous weather the day of my wedding?" Piper wondered as she backed the truck into a vendor's parking spot on Friday morning. She turned to face Rainey before they crossed the grass lot to the festival area. "Remember, if you need me, I'm in the booth next door. I've got your back. Okay?"

Rainey waved off her concerns and swallowed the urge to run far and fast. "I'm fine. A little nervous, but I've got Marly and cinnamon milk. What more could I need?"

"That amazingly good-looking sheriff's deputy who has set his sights on us from over there?" Marly indicated the petting zoo across from their booth.

Luke headed toward them with a cardboard tray of fresh-baked apple fritters from the Barretts' stand. "Consider this breakfast," he said as they met at the corner of the McKinney booth. "Or lunch. If we're as busy as the town expects, it might be both."

"Thank you. I'll devour some once I'm set." Rainey grinned up at him, then hurried into the booth to double-check her coolers.

She and Marly set up the basket display on the shady side of the booth. By the time the festival opened, they were stocked, decorated, organized, and both booths looked great.

Customers came sporadically at first, but as the temperature rose, more people stopped to check things out. By lunchtime Rainey was feeling less nervous. Some folks were avoiding her purposely, but the booth's steady business said she was doing something right.

"*Tres leches* cakes?" A nice-looking man stopped by in the early afternoon and studied her samples with a look more intent than most. "In different flavors? What a great idea."

"Try some." Rainey held out the tray of samples. "See which you prefer. Coconut lovers have an obvious favorite, but the traditional cake and the apple eggnog variety are making plenty of folks happy."

"I will, thanks." He sampled each one, and Rainey sensed he wasn't simply tasting the combinations, his expression said the cakes passed the test. "I'm not sure I have a favorite because they're all wonderful. You made these yourself?" he asked.

"Using my Mexican grandmother's recipe," she explained. "I think the texture is perfect. Not too light, not too dense."

"Exactly." His appreciation mirrored her thoughts. "Not too many people understand that balance. You'll be selling these at the store?"

"Yes. We wanted to introduce them here and then carry them in the store for take-out and special orders."

"Excellent." He leaned forward and stretched out his hand. "Greg Barrett from Barrett's Orchards. My sister came to see you last night."

"Of course." Rainey shook his hand, then held on. "And I want you to know that your family is in our prayers."

"Thank you." He turned as Luke came up alongside him. "Luke, how are you?"

Luke clasped the other man's hand in a grip that showed friendship. "Good, Greg. Nice to have you back, but my condolences on your father. I'll miss the way he loved being out on the water in the summer. His laugh. That sense of humor. Tom Barrett always had something to laugh about. We loved that about him."

Greg's face showed a raw mix of emotions. "He's had a rough go of it these past few months. Right now having God call him home will be a blessing and a sorrow."

"No one's ever quite ready to say goodbye," Rainey added.

"That's true," Greg admitted. "Well, I must get going. Lacey asked me to stop and check out our booth, make sure the crew has everything they need. Dad insisted we do this, even though he's taken a turn." Greg made a face. "Stubborn to the end. But we weren't about to argue with him."

Rainey sent him a look of commiseration. "My mother would be the same way, so I understand. You go. And God bless you all."

"Thank you. And I'd like to give you a call about the cakes." He handed her his card. "I'm thinking we could do an exclusive flavor at the lodge, one that people can't get at the store. And once I've settled into the job there, I'd like to carry your dairy products in the kitchen. If we did a standing order twice a week, could you deliver?"

Another sales venue for the dairy store. Rainey smiled calmly while her heart did a salsa dance in her chest. "Of course. And I'd love to develop a cake flavor for you. Maybe we could do seasonal ones, as well."

People were gathering at the stand, so Greg stepped back to make room. "Give me a call and we can talk." He shifted his gaze to Luke and stuck out his hand once more. "Good to see you, pal."

"You, too."

"They're a nice family, Luke." Rainey refilled a tray and handed it to Marly, who was offering samples. "You grew up together?"

He nodded. "There was a crowd of us. We hung out, did youth group together, had some of the same classes, but then we grew up. Went our separate ways," he added. "Oops, I've got a nursery school crew coming my way. I'm going to go protect tiny four-legged creatures. And a few chickens."

"You do that." She grinned, but his words hit a nerve. Lacey Barrett's name was listed in the local church bulletin as a musician. Sean Barrett headed the youth group.

The obvious truth rose up before her. Luke didn't see them anymore because he never went to church. Their paths didn't cross because Luke was busy working and raising Aiden, which didn't include church attendance or prayer. She should have seen this before, but Aiden and the girls talked so naturally about God and faith that she hadn't recognized the obvious. Aiden knew about God from his grandmother, an ardent member of the church. Not from his father. Because he didn't attend church. Or talk about God. Or embrace faith.

A bus of senior citizens from Clearwater pulled up alongside the festival grounds. Rainey put her thoughts on hold. Frankly, that was better than dwelling on what she'd just realized: that Luke Campbell didn't practice the faith he was raised in.

Rainey did. She knew what the absence of faith had wrought in her life. She'd lived the emptiness and longing. The lure of bad choices. She was stronger now because she was steeped in the spirit. And there was no way she'd ever compromise her faith again.

Strangers mobbed Rainey's booth, so her sales would be healthy, Luke noted later that afternoon. Folks were sampling tiny cups of the cakes and milks, then ordering larger versions. She'd do okay by the numbers.

But the attitude of some locals indicated she still had a fight on her hands.

When Laura Spelling's eldest son walked by, he snarled something under his breath.

Marly looked shocked.

Rainey drew a breath and went on working the crowd with a smile.

When the Cosgroves brought their preschool grandchildren to see the kids and lambs, Mrs. Cosgrove made it clear, in a voice meant to be overheard, that they'd avoid the opposite side of the path.

And when a seedy-looking guy stopped by Rainey's booth to talk over old times, Luke had to fight the urge to send the guy packing.

But he didn't need to. Rainey's kindness accomplished the task. The guy walked off, looking surprised and annoyed, but when he glanced back, Luke saw something else in his expression, as if whatever Rainey had said made a difference.

He turned toward Piper's booth, knowing she and Marty were watching over Rainey, too. They exchanged looks, and Piper raised her shoulders in a shrug, but her expression said she was proud of her sister.

So was Luke.

But when he arrived at the festival grounds early Saturday morning, he stared at Rainey's booth, horrified.

Crude graffiti covered the freshly painted surfaces. Nasty words scrawled in permanent black marker insulted Rainey in every way possible. Her beautiful decorations were stripped away; bundles of colorful Indian corn lay broken and strewn in the walking path. Her pretty swags and wreaths had been torn to pieces and scattered about. Everything was gone. Ruined. The booth that Aiden, Sonya and Dorrie had worked so hard on was unrecognizable.

Piper's truck pulled in. Luke wanted to shield Rainey from this venomous attack, but when she and Piper climbed out of the cab with Zach's sister Julia, he saw that they carried a long roll of plain white paper and tape.

"You know?" He crossed the field to meet them and took the heavy roll from Rainey's arms.

"Seth called us. He's on early patrol and saw what they did, so we came prepared." Rainey stared at the booth. For just a moment her chin quivered, but then she directed Luke to set the roll of paper on the table. "Julia, you cut. Piper and I will window-dress this garbage. If we hurry, we can have it all covered before the festival opens."

Luke got his animals settled while the women worked.

As other vendors streamed in to set up, he saw them note the commotion in Rainey's space, and an odd thing happened. While some appeared satisfied, as if Rainey had gotten her just due, others came by to help. And more soon followed.

"I've got a nice stepladder so we can reach those high places," offered one older gentleman. "I'll be right back."

"And I've got plenty of decorations to share from my spot," said a middle-aged woman from Clearwater. "Once you've covered this mess, we'll get you decorated pretty again."

"I'd be grateful," Rainey told her.

Luckily, Rainey's food had been trucked back home, and the gift baskets had been stored in a second truck overnight. But the booth itself had been vandalized in every other way possible.

It took over an hour, but by the time the festival opened, Rainey's display looked welcoming again. No one would know that dark, angry words lurked beneath the heavy-duty paper. And the donations from other vendors made Rainey's area look more festive than it had the day before.

"Folks should mind their own business," one man told Rainey as he stood on the borrowed ladder to affix bunting to the upper reaches of the booth. "There's no call to be wrecking stuff."

"I agree." Mrs. Thurgood had come by to lay out crocheted doilies where Rainey's trays would go. "You set those delicious cakes on here, honey. It'll be pretty as a picture again."

"Thank you, Mrs. Thurgood." Rainey came around the corner of the dairy stand. Gratitude softened her features. "Thank you so much."

"Bah." Mary Thurgood waved off her thanks. "Rainey, I've been around a long time and I love my town, but there's always folks that forget to live what they hear preached on Sunday. And that's a shame. Don't you go thinking you deserved this," the old woman scolded.

The look on Rainey's face told Luke the words hit home.

"Do you remember the woman in the Bible?" Mrs. Thurgood asked. "About to be stoned for making a mistake? Jesus reminded folks that we're all sinners. We all make mistakes. It's what we do after those mistakes that counts. I know you risked your life to get those bad cops off the streets, and I'm grateful."

Rainey's eyes watered at her words, but she blinked them back as a middle-aged vendor from Warrentown came by with more contributions. "Here, honey, use these on your tables."

"Thank you." Rainey hugged her and Mrs. Thurgood as Luke finished cleaning the pathway. "I appreciate your help. But mostly your kind words."

"Just bein' neighborly," Mary Thurgood assured her. "And I'd like a bottle of that cinnamon milk to keep for later. It's an old favorite of mine and I was so excited to see you carrying it yesterday. And two slices of the coconut cake."

"And I'll take the same, only I'd like the apple eggnog cake," said the other woman. "Three pieces, please. One for each of my daughters."

When Rainey tried to refuse their money, the women fussed at her. She gave in, and looked around as Luke leaned his big rake against a fence post. "I can't believe this."

"I know."

She shook her head and motioned to the beautiful booth. "Not the damage. I half expected someone to act stupid. But the help. The support. The donations people made to help me. I prayed for God to tell me what to do. Know how to fix things. For Him to make me strong. And then this happened."

Luke shrugged. "There are nice people everywhere, Rainey. Sometimes the negative ones are noisier, but I think most folks try to be good."

"Well, it was an answer to prayer," she said lightly. "I couldn't have the kids see that stuff. As of now, I'm putting it behind me."

That was easier said than done, but Luke read the determination in her eyes and knew she was in it for the long haul.

She is. Should you be?

The question made Luke think hard as he tended the miniature goats.

She's strong. She's tough. And she has no choice but to meet things head-on if she wants to prove herself. But you and Aiden have done nothing wrong. Today, graffitti. Tomorrow? Who knows? You've got a five-year-old kid who's been through the mill already. He's just getting his feet set on solid ground. What if someone confronts Rainey with Aiden around?

Was he right to put an innocent five-year-old boy in the middle of such angst? Cops were wolves, guarding the sheep. He knew what the darker side of humanity could do. Today's destruction was a minimal version of what could happen. He hated that Rainey was targeted. But Hillary's words came back to him…. Was he putting Aiden first now? Or himself?

Luke wasn't sure anymore.

Chapter Twelve

By the time she got the girls to bed that night, Rainey was exhausted. Lucia motioned for her to sit down, and she did, then accepted the cup of hot tea her mother gave her. "I'm wiped."

Lucia's expression was understanding. "So many long days in a row, and then good sales! You should be proud, Larraina. But that nasty business makes me worry. There might be some who will not stop at messing up a booth. People might hurt you, or the girls. And then I wonder at what cost do we try to fix things here?"

Rainey leaned forward. "I've wondered about this, too. And I pray about it constantly. I still feel like I'm meant to be here, Mama. Things will be made right eventually. I don't want to endanger the girls or make people mad. But I want to belong, so I'm going to stick it out. I think we made good headway this weekend, and that's what I wanted to do."

"And I believe that our town saw what some are capable of," Lucia mused. "That might help, as well."

"The children had fun today," Rainey told her. "Luke let them help with the petting zoo. And his parents took them around the festival midday and let them play games and eat wonderful things. They even took a wagon ride through town with Ben Hull's draft horses."

"The girls will sleep well. Me, too." Lucia rose, hugged Rainey and padded off toward bed. "I will see you in the morning."

"All right." Luke had invited the girls over to play tomorrow, but Rainey had gently refused. After several hectic weeks, she thought a quiet day at the farm was in order.

But there was another reason she'd begged off. A niggle of awareness had nudged her again that morning, when she'd talked to Luke about God answering her prayer.

He'd brushed it off.

And that had made her think hard.

Luke didn't go to church with his family. He didn't take Aiden to church. He didn't talk about God or faith except in the past tense.

Not all Christians were churchgoers. Rainey respected that. Folks were entitled to keep their faith their own way. But the thought of *no* faith…

Heart heavy, she went to bed, knowing she and Luke needed to have a serious discussion. She'd come too far with God's help to take life and love casually. Her faith sustained her, and she wouldn't take that lightly. She went to bed, praying she was wrong, knowing she wasn't. And she hated how much that hurt.

"Hillary." Luke finished feeding the ewe and her rapidly growing lambs as his sister-in-law approached him from the driveway Sunday afternoon. "I wasn't expecting you."

"I know. I'm pretty sure I'm not welcome here right now, but I had to talk to you."

She drew a deep breath and studied the barn and the animal pens, but Luke suspected she wasn't seeing them. She was going back three years to that dreadful day when her sister had disappeared. "I heard what they did to your girlfriend's booth at the festival."

His girlfriend. Put that way, it sounded sophomoric, which may have been what Hillary intended. Was Rainey his girlfriend?

No, she was more. But how could she be more after so short a time?

"Yes?"

"I've handled this whole thing badly," Hillary confessed. "And that's my fault for wanting to fix things for you. And for me. The thought of Martha gone makes me crazy sometimes, even after all this time. It shouldn't, should it, Luke? But every holiday, every birthday, every special occasion seems wrong without her here to share it."

Her expression said more than her words. She wanted absolution, to be forgiven for her sister's choice. So did he. Only it wasn't forthcoming. "Me, too."

"Really?" Her single word said his honesty helped. "Because you're always so strong. So focused. I've been clinging to that, to you and Aiden, because I can't talk to our parents. They want to blame someone, anyone, and they're still full of questions that have no answers. I can't handle that talk anymore. I started going to a therapist last week."

Luke nodded.

"I realized I wasn't helping things by babying Aiden, that you were right about that—"

"You mean *Rainey* was right."

Her face went still as she contemplated his words, but eventually she went on. "I guess. But I want you to know I respect your choices with Aiden. You're his father and I know you want what's best for him. But then when I heard what happened at the festival, I wondered where Aiden fit into this whole thing."

She waved a hand toward the west shore. "What if the next time people don't stop at vandalism? What if her old crowd targets you? Or Aiden? I heard some of them are angry because the girl that really held up the convenience store will probably go to jail. It might have been a long time ago, but the sins of the past come back to haunt us, Luke. Are you willing to risk your son?"

She stepped back. "I'm not telling you what to do, but there are a lot of people still angry with what Rainey's friends did back then. And they don't think much of mothers leaving their children for years, either. I just wanted you to know I'm sorry for what happened at your parents' place, and I'll make sure it never happens again. And I'm asking you if you'll let me see Aiden now and again. Please?"

Luke hated to say no, but he wasn't sure about saying yes, either. "Aiden loves you, Hillary," he admitted. "You'll always be his aunt. But you have to be willing to let him grow up. Try new things. And you can't talk badly about Rainey around him. Ever. Being a deputy puts me in in touch with some sketchy characters every day, from hard-core criminals to low-life vandals. In all my years I don't think I've ever met a person with a truer heart than Rainey's, regardless of her past. Yes, she's made mistakes. But so have we. Right?"

Hillary's face showed doubt, but she shrugged. "Some mistakes are more serious than others, Luke."

He knew that. He'd married a woman who'd chosen death over life with him. With their son. He swallowed hard and faced her. "If you want to see Aiden, it's got to be on my terms, Hillary. Are you all right with that?"

"I am."

Luke nodded. "We'll set something up. He's doing a Thanksgiving play and then a Christmas concert at school. You and your parents are welcome to come, of course. But if you and your folks want to take him for a little while over Thanksgiving, we'll arrange that. Saturday of that weekend would be good for me. Okay?"

Her expression said his offer fell short of what she wanted, but she accepted it gracefully. "Yes. I'll talk with Mom and Dad and we'll plan a fun day for him. Thank you, Luke."

He finished taking care of the animals once she'd left, then went inside to wash up before going to his parents' for dinner.

Hillary wanted to make amends. Could he trust her to be discreet about her feelings for Rainey?

She'd raised a valid point. What if someone targeted Aiden in an attempt to hurt Rainey? Rainey had friends and enemies on both sides of the law. Her old crowd thought of her as a traitor. The police force saw her as a helper, because she'd blown the lid on a rough crime ring of cops, mobsters and politicians. But that meant there were still people who might like to see Rainey suffer. Would those people act out on innocent children?

He didn't know, but he'd seen the destruction at the festival, and he'd been a cop a long time. For some folks, vandalism was as far as they'd go. For others it was a stepping stone. Luke wasn't sure which they were dealing with. Recognizing that, was he wrong to put his son in harm's way?

Yes.

Did that mean he should give up thoughts of a future with Rainey? With her girls? Would they all be better off apart?

Probably. But that didn't mean he wanted it.

Rainey dialed the pastor's number once the girls were in bed that night. She needed unbiased advice, and the reverend and his wife had been good to her from her first day back. He answered and didn't seem surprised to have her call him on a Sunday evening. "Reverend Smith, it's Rainey McKinney. Do you have some time?"

"I was just telling Mother that company would be a nice thing tonight. Come straight over."

His graciousness warmed her. She was pretty sure he and Mrs. Smith would have enjoyed a quiet Sunday evening on their own, but his invitation meant a great deal to Rainey. "I'll be right there." She drove to the lakeside village, parked her mother's car in the church lot and walked up to the small, unassuming rectory.

"I've put water on for tea." Mrs. Smith shepherded Rainey into the house, settled her on a sofa, then set a box of tissues and a plate of cookies on the table in front of her. "Covering all the bases, dear." She smiled at the cookies and tissues. "Most folks appreciate both."

"Thank you, Mrs. Smith. And you don't have to go," Rainey told her. "I don't have anything to say that you can't both hear."

Mrs. Smith sent her husband a questioning look.

"It's fine, dear. Sit with us. So, Rainey." Reverend Smith sat down and leaned forward, hands clenched. "Let me start off by saying you've already come further than anyone thought, and quicker, too. So no matter what's on your mind, Mother and I want you to know we're glad you're back. And we're proud of you."

Their kindness softened her heart, but she had known both of them since childhood. They were also honest and direct, two qualities she needed right now. "I have a problem."

The pastor nodded. "Go ahead."

"You know me. You understand how far I sank into the abyss. But I've worked hard to hang on to God, faith, work and common sense. I've tried to become the daughter my mother deserved all along, but now I'm at a bend in the road."

The pastor's eyes invited her to continue. She sighed, clasped her hands and met their looks of compassion. "I'm in love with Luke Campbell."

Reverend Smith exchanged a glance with his wife and rubbed a hand to his jaw. "Luke is a good man."

"He is. But he's not a believer. He has no faith.

And I can't enter into a serious relationship with someone who doesn't share my beliefs in God."

"But you *want* to enter a serious relationship with him?" Mrs. Smith asked, and Rainey nodded.

"Yes. I keep holding back, knowing it's wrong, knowing I need to follow God's word and my conscience." She stared at her hands, then raised her gaze to theirs. "My heart longs for him. He's funny, he's kind, he's so nice to the girls that it makes my heart ache in a good way. But I can't pretend that faith isn't important to me. That I can live side by side with a man who doesn't believe as I do. I know what I was before I clung to God. I can't risk going back there again. Even for Luke."

"Ah, Rainey." The pastor's grimace said he had no easy answers. "You have so much goodness inside you—"

Rainey scoffed lightly, but he pressed on. "You do. You have always had a giving spirit, but you were such an angry child. Angry at your mother for having you, angry about not having a father. And then you got mad at her for bringing you here from Texas, for changing everything in your life. She didn't know how to channel that anger, and you drifted apart."

"I remember."

"But do you also remember that in your anger, you still protected others? First, that girl who robbed the store. You took her place in jail so she could have her baby in freedom."

"A baby that was never born," Rainey reminded him, but the pastor waved that off.

"You didn't know that. You took the noble road at great personal cost. You are no stranger to self-lessness. We recognize that." He nodded to his wife. "Lucia knows that, as well. Others will understand in time. But to jump into a relationship with Luke could have serious consequences. He is still wrestling with guilt and anger over his wife's death."

The pastor was right. Rainey had seen the despair in Luke's face. Martha's death had hit him hard.

"He is very protective of those he loves, but in your case, that could become a problem for both of you. I would like nothing better than to say yes, go forth, and be married, but I don't dare. Not knowing you as I do."

"Because of my weaknesses."

"No, Rainey." He shook his head and his expression became grave. "Because of his. And until he comes to grips with the past, I don't believe Luke can fully love in the present."

The reverend was right. She hated the truth, but it couldn't be denied, so she grabbed a clump of Mrs. Smith's tissues, dried the tears that had tracked down her cheeks, and hauled in a deep, cleansing breath. "So. What do I do?"

The pastor leaned forward earnestly. "You do exactly what you've been doing, child. You pray. God chooses the unlikely for a reason."

She frowned at him.

"Surrounded by tax collectors, traitors, women of the streets and fishermen. Oh, yes." The pastor's smile widened. "He chooses the unlikely most frequently, and with good results. You hang on to your faith, and we'll pray right along with you. Our vision may be limited, but God sees around those bends in the road."

Rainey knew she needed to ease away from Luke, and she'd avoided that conversation on purpose. But no more. She was strong, with or without Luke Campbell in her life. She just really wished it could have been with him.

"You're avoiding me, Rain, but I didn't get this badge by being a pushover, so I will keep calling. And stopping by. Aiden and I miss you and the girls."

Luke hadn't seen Rainey or talked to her in days, and his call had gone straight to voice mail, again.

He'd texted her about getting the kids together. She'd texted back that they were busy.

He'd stopped by the dairy store, but Rainey wasn't there. He'd gone to the house, had coffee with Lucia and brought home a loaf of banana bread she gave him, but he didn't see Rainey.

He missed her. It had been less than a week apart,

but he longed to talk with her. Laugh with her. Listen to her words of wisdom. Her commonsense approach brightened his days. November was bleak in Western New York, the skies leaden with clouds off Lake Erie. Time with Rainey made the gray days less dreary.

He'd used up his days off to provide the petting zoo at the festival, and he was scheduled to patrol that weekend. That left little time to figure things out with her. But then a text from Rainey came through in the early afternoon. Please meet me at your house after work.

Luke's heart tightened.

She'd avoided him and now suddenly wanted to talk to him alone, without the kids around. That didn't bode well. But he'd rather talk than deal with silence. He'd done that with Martha, the long days of quiet, the weeks of sadness, months of emotional separation. He'd dealt with it the best he could, but it hadn't been enough.

Guilt speared him. He'd loved Martha, but he'd let her down. Maybe he was foolish to risk caring again. He had Aiden to consider.

You have yourself to consider. You messed up once. What makes you think you can get it right this time, especially with Rainey?

He knew his limits better than most, and he still wanted a second chance. Did that make him weak, to desire happiness? Or did it make him selfish?

He drove home after work, wishing he could change things. Her past meant nothing to him, because the woman he cared about—the woman he loved—was the grown-up Rainey, not a teenage kid with anger issues. Surely that would be enough.

"Hey." A strong west wind had blown in. Rainey pulled her coat tighter and dashed up the steps to Luke's side door, the covered porch saving her from the strongest gusts of sleet. "I'm glad we could meet."

His expression said her words made little sense. "Me, too, except I've been trying to get hold of you all week and you've been putting me off. What's going on, Rain?"

Her heart softened at the way he said her name. She toughened it again, knowing her choices were limited, wishing they weren't.

"Would you like coffee? Or tea?" He motioned to the brewing system on his kitchen countertop.

"No." She bit her lip, grabbed his hand and drew him into the living room. "Let's sit. I'm nervous enough and standing is making it worse."

"All right." He sat across from her and leaned forward. "What's up?"

"We started seeing each other because of the kids," she began, but he interrupted her.

"Except we knew there was more between us at the time. We just didn't want to admit it."

"Yes." She accepted the truth in his words. "Which is why I set up those first rules, which we managed to break within days."

His smile broadened. "I like breaking rules with you, Rain. Just thinking about it makes me happy."

She knew what he meant. Being together. Holding hands. Stealing a kiss. Enjoying a warm embrace. She'd felt so safe in his arms.

She drew in a breath and let it out. "But we can't do that any longer, Luke. Our children love each other, and they're good for each other, but you and I live in different worlds and that can't be in anyone's best interests."

"Because you broke the law when you were a kid, and I'm a cop?" He scoffed at the idea. "That's silly, Rainey. That was a long time ago. It's over. Done."

"Not that." She fingered the tiny cross she wore around her neck. "I came to terms with my past. I made peace with God and my family. I came back to Kirkwood Lake ready to begin a new life, no matter what happens."

"Then why not begin that life together?" He stood, paced the room, then came back to stand in front of her. Gently, he bent and reached for her hand. "Why not share your life with me? Let us start fresh, a new family?"

Tears filled her eyes. She'd known this wouldn't be easy, but did it have to be this hard? He was offering her his love, his life, his home, his son. It would be so easy to turn a blind eye to God and relax into this good man's embrace. The Bible made it clear that God wanted his people happy. Couldn't she cling to that verse? Seeing Luke's inviting look of love tempted her.

Common sense held her back. "We don't share a faith, Luke." She tried to keep her voice even, but a hint of old emotion crept in. "And I remember the person I was without faith."

"You were a kid, Rainey," he argued. "We all make mistakes when we're kids. Can't we move beyond that together?"

She shook her head, trying to stave off the tears and failing. "I can't. I know you don't understand it, and I'll pray for you all my days, but I can't risk all that I've gained. I love you."

His face shadowed with disbelief as she covered their joined hands with her free one.

"But we can only be friends, Luke."

His heart seized.

He knew what she wanted. The request was scrawled across her face, darkening her eyes, flowing in her tears, imploring him to understand.

She wanted him to cling to God, as she did. But just as he couldn't take Aiden's hand in a prayer before meals, he couldn't pretend to have faith. "I can't meet you halfway on that ground, Rainey. I know what you'd like, the picture-perfect family that goes to church on Sunday and prays together. But I can't live a lie. How can I pretend to believe? I can't, any more than you would want me to."

"I know." She nodded and stood. Drew a breath as if fighting to stay calm. Silent tears snaked paths down her cheeks, and his heart broke, knowing he couldn't give her what she wanted. "I wouldn't want you to fake it, either."

He stepped forward, wanting to stop her tears. Hold her. Embrace her. Make everything all right. "Why is it so important, Rain? Why does it make such a difference to you?"

She stood straighter, leaned up and kissed his cheek in a quiet farewell. "That's what I'll be praying for, Luke. That someday you understand why it makes a difference." She pulled her hands from his and moved toward the door. "We can still have the kids get together, if you want to. You can drop Aiden at our place or I can drop the girls off here."

"Kids only."

She nodded. "Yes."

He wanted to throw something, but cops didn't give in to fits of temper. They couldn't afford to. He stayed where he was and shrugged. "I'll need time to think on that."

"Of course."

That was what weeks of hopes and dreams boiled down to. Two simple words of assent that meant nothing.

She walked out the door and through the wind and icy rain to the waiting car. She walked slowly, lost in thought.

No, she's praying, numbskull.

Luke had prayed. He'd begged. He'd promised anything God required, and got nothing in return, so forgive him for washing his hands of the whole God thing.

At the car door, Rainey turned and faced the house. Her gaze swept his home as though wondering, longing, hoping.

And then she climbed into Lucia's aging Camry, and drove away.

Chapter Thirteen

Luke wrote more speeding tickets in November than should have been humanly possible. He volunteered for all the overtime he could get and pretended it was okay to leave Aiden with his grandma so often.

His heart ached. Stress headaches invaded his sleep.

He didn't take Aiden to see the girls. He couldn't do that, couldn't pretend to be just friends with Rainey McKinney when what he really wanted was to change her name and offer her a new address in his hillside home above Kirkwood Lake.

He glared at each church he passed, angered by the sheer number of them in the small, lakeside communities. And when Thanksgiving came, he clasped hands around his parents' table and felt nothing but gut-wrenching anger with his father's gentle prayer of thanks.

"Luke, did you find someone to watch Aiden this Saturday?" Jenny asked after dinner. "I'd watch him if I could, but Dad's store will be busy and he'll need me on hand."

"Hillary's taking him to her parents' place for the day," he told her. "This will give them some holiday time together. He's going to help Martha's parents decorate for Christmas." He tried not to choke on the word. Right now the thought of Christmas without Rainey and the girls loomed lifeless and glum. But he'd have to get a clue for his son's sake, because Aiden deserved his full attention.

"I want to go see Sonya and Dorrie this weekend," Aiden announced. "I haven't gotten to play with them in weeks!" He shoved his chair back from the table and stood.

"You see them in school every day," Luke remarked quietly.

"It's not the same, Dad."

It wasn't. Luke knew that. They were living each day as a pale reminder of what could have been, and the loss of that hope needled him daily.

His mother jumped in to ward off the battle brewing between father and son. "Helping Grandma and Grandpa Baxter will be nice, Aiden." She shot him a look of approval. "They love spending time with you."

Aiden stomped off, unconvinced, and Jenny turned toward Luke, but his father motioned him over to the noisy television room just then. "Luke. Seth. Have you guys seen this weather alert?"

Luke crossed to the sunken family room. Bold orange stripes scrolled across the bottom of the screen, warning of an approaching storm front. The meteorologists' map showed two storms converging over Western New York. "This could be bad," he muttered. "We've had nearly three weeks of rain already. A long, drenching storm with sustained winds could mean serious flooding in the southern basin."

"Which means we'll be sleeping at the barracks," Seth announced.

"They'll be setting up sandbag groups now," their father speculated. "Luke, check it out, see if they need bags. The Army Corps of Engineers might have some nearby, but I have a pallet of them at the hardware store. If they can send a truck up, we can load them this afternoon and get them to the south shore before the storm actually hits."

Luke called command, made his father's offer, and they had a reply within minutes. "Truck's on the way. They said payment might take a while."

Charlie brushed that off. "Payments come eventually. I bought these just in case we had an emergency. There's never time to get them if you wait for things to happen."

His words etched Luke's heart.

Was that what he'd been doing these last years?

Waiting for things to happen instead of moving on, embracing life with his son?

"I'll meet you at the store, Dad." Seth jingled his keys as he headed for the door. "I've got to get stuff from my place. Mom, feel free to pack up a couple of pies for the crew. They'd love it, and Luke and I might not see you for a few days. I'd hate to see that chocolate cream go to waste."

She waved him on. "Go get your stuff. I'll have the pies ready to go when you guys get back here."

"I'll ride with you, Seth." Luke followed his brother to his SUV. "No sense taking three cars."

"Sounds good."

As the Campbell men piled into Charlie's truck and Seth's car, Luke had no time to think further about his dad's words. If this storm mushroomed like the computer models showed, he'd be on duty day and night until the emergency passed, catching catnaps on hard cots in the barracks.

"We're in for a heck of a Thanksgiving weekend," Seth remarked.

Luke frowned. "So it seems."

"And since I'm dreading this whole holiday thing, I'm looking forward to being so busy I can't think about what Tori's doing. If she's happy. If her mother's new boyfriend is good to her."

Guilt struck Luke hard. His brother had been going through a rough time since his wife left him nearly two years ago. Last Christmas had been tough on him, but Luke had assumed this one would be better. That time had helped heal the ache in Seth's big heart. It was a stupid assumption because he knew how painful the holidays were after he lost Martha.

You didn't lose her. She left you. You and your son. You got dumped just like Seth, but in a different way.

As they wound through the village to Seth's historic home, Christmas lights brightened up the darkening afternoon. The village roads crew had attached illuminated wreaths to each lamppost. Twinkle lights blanketed every tree. Storefronts, ready for tomorrow's start to the holiday season, featured Christmas displays of toys, villages and winter scenes.

For the first time in years, Luke had been looking forward to celebrating Christmas. The beautiful town gave him another harsh look in the mirror.

He'd barely decorated for the holiday. His mother kept up the traditions Aiden had come to know and love. Making cookies. Setting up the crèche. Stringing popcorn and cranberries to wrap around the big tree his father complained about every year.

While smiling at his wife across the room.

Luke wanted to shove this Christmas aside, too, but it was time for him to make things special for his son. What had he been thinking these last three years? Passing through the picturesque village, he promised himself he'd do whatever it took to make Aiden's holidays special. Luke was only sorry he'd wasted so much time.

He couldn't think about Rainey, about her first Christmas back home with the girls. He pushed thoughts of her and the twins away. Keeping busy was more appealing than feeling sorry for himself, and the incoming storm might break the anger he'd clung to since Rainey had walked out that door. Because more than anything, he wanted her to say it had been a mistake and promise they could work things out.

But three long, silent weeks later, he understood that wasn't going to happen. No matter how much he wished for it.

Chapter Fourteen

"Mommy, can we play with Aiden today?" Sonya asked Saturday, her soft voice beseeching.

"We haven't played with him in forever!" Dorrie's righteous indignation and the vigorous foot-stomping highlighted the differences between the twins.

"Not today, ladies. I think his daddy is working because of the storm." She assumed that was true. She'd texted Luke twice in the past few weeks, offering playdates for the kids, and got short negative replies for her trouble.

He was right to refuse. She knew that. Even seeing him from time to time, dropping the kids off, would make it hard to step fully away, so kudos to him for being the strong one.

She got out a Lite-Brite her mother had found at a garage sale and turned the girls loose with the colorful acrylic pegs and the lighted board. As the storm raged around them, she took time to sit and pray.

The store's business had mushroomed over the last week. She'd filled dozens of orders for cakes, and they'd sold nearly as much cinnamon milk as they did eggnog.

Her head celebrated the success.

Her heart longed for Luke. She thought it would get easier with time, but the approaching holidays warned otherwise. As she strung twinkle lights in the farmhouse windows, she wondered if Luke would bother to decorate for Aiden. Would he see how perfect a crèche would look on his side table? Did he have garlands to loop along the pretty front porch? Would he bother with a wreath for the thick oak door?

Stop torturing yourself. Move on. This Christmas you should be celebrating your family, your faith, your homecoming. Trust God in all things, but grasp what you've been given. It's so much more than you had before.

She would listen to her conscience. Trust her instincts. God had delivered her from evil and given her joy in the form of two blessed girls who'd grown to love her. No matter what, she needed to appreciate that blessing.

The house phone rang. She saw Luke's number in the caller ID, hesitated, then picked up, but it wasn't Luke on the other end. It was Hillary, crying. Hysterical.

"Aiden's gone. He got mad at me because he

wanted to go to your house and he couldn't, and Luke's fighting the flood in the river valley, and I called the police but the weather is so bad, and he's so little, and what if he's trying to get to your house and he's hit by a car?"

Aiden. Ran away from home?

Guilt broadsided Rainey. They should have prepared for this. They'd worked to make the little boy more assertive and independent, so why wouldn't he strike out on his own when the adults around him did foolish things? "I'll be right there. My mother's here. If he makes it around the lake, she'll be here to welcome him."

Hillary's sobs were the last thing Rainey heard as she disconnected. She grabbed her boots, her hoodie and one of Piper's farm coats, checked the pockets for waterproof gloves, found them, and headed for the door. She waggled her phone at her mother. "I'll explain from the car, gotta go."

The gravity in Lucia's face said more than words. "I will be here, waiting."

As Rainey popped the car into gear, she thought of what her mother had said. That's what she'd aspired to those years in Illinois. To become the kind of mother who withstood crisis after crisis, waiting. Praying. A port in the storm. It took years on her own for Rainey to realize what she'd had, and how she'd misused her mother's love.

Now she wanted nothing more than to emulate it.

She called Lucia on the phone so the twins wouldn't overhear what was happening, and rued every extra minute it took to get to Luke's place in the teeming rain. Twice she had to ease around tree branches in the road, but eventually she made it, hopped out of the car and onto Luke's porch.

Hillary opened the door quickly. A gust caught the storm door, and the force of the wind slammed it into Rainey's face. "Oh my gosh, I'm sorry. So sorry!"

Rainey shook her head, her cheek stinging from the unexpected slap of metal. "Doesn't matter. Tell me what you know."

"Nothing. He was mad and went to his room, and I was playing solitaire on the computer. I went to check on him, thinking he fell asleep, and he was gone. His window was open and I could see footprints in the mud."

"Which way?"

Hillary pointed south. "Down the hill. But there were only a few prints, so maybe he didn't go that way at all."

"You checked the barn?"

"Yes. Well. Kind of. Not, like, up the ladder."

Rainey bit back words of recrimination. Not everyone was raised on a farm, or accustomed to crawling through straw stacks and meeting four-footed little critters eye to eye. "What did the police say?"

"They're overwhelmed with the storm and they've got emergencies everywhere, but they said they'd swarm the area to look for Luke's son. Again."

Again. Because Luke's son had been lost once before. That time he'd survived, tucked inside a car. Now, with two days of pouring rain, out in the cold?

God help Aiden.

Rainey didn't want to hug Hillary. She didn't want to befriend a woman whose shallow dislike fed others' anger. But she'd never lost a sister to suicide or spent days combing the hills, looking for a small child. Aiden's disappearance would push old buttons. Bring up difficult losses. And for that she reached out, hugged Hillary and headed back out. "My mother will call if he shows up there. The roads are bad, so it might take the sheriffs in the southern sector a while to get here. I'm going to check the barns. If he's not here, I'll take a horse out and look. Stay by the phone and pray, Hillary. Pray hard. And if you belong to a prayer chain, get them involved."

A spark of hope lit Hillary's eyes. "I will. Right now."

Rainey ran to the barn. Luke's barns were ridiculously clean, so it didn't take her long to decide Aiden wasn't there. She headed to the horse stalls, eyed the three pensioners and reached for the latch on one door. "Come here, Star, I'm going to need your help."

Spirit stomped in the stall next door.

Rainey met his gaze as she undid Star's latch. "Hey, old boy."

Stomp! Stomp! He shook his head at her, and the look in the old horse's eyes said he wondered why she'd consider taking an everyday mare out on a search when she had a trained deputy nearby.

The horse had a point. She studied him, then Star, then relatched the door. "You want to go?"

Spirit nodded. He pawed the ground as if understanding time was of the essence. Rainey disregarded the craziness of her decision, opened Spirit's stall and got him saddled in record time. She walked him out of the barn.

He sniffed, head high, then pawed the ground with his right hoof, telling her to mount up. She took a breath, put one foot in the stirrup, grabbed the horn and hauled herself up and over. Spirit's size didn't make mounting easy, but once astride, she loved the feel of the powerful horse beneath her. Nothing dainty about the sixteen-hand, twelve-hundred-pound Morgan cross. She leaned down and whispered in his ear. "We've got to find Aiden, old boy. The roads are wet and the hills are slippery. But we can do this together."

His head bob was all she needed. They started down the southern slope, Spirit picking his way, getting a feel for the ground.

They had only a few hours before dark. A few short hours of daylight before a five-year-old boy would be lost overnight. No way was Rainey about to let that happen.

She urged Spirit into the woods leading toward the creek ravine.

She found nothing.

She called Aiden's name until her voice went raw. No response.

Her phone rang. Hillary was calling. Rainey answered promptly. "Nothing yet. Spirit and I are on the southeast side, heading toward the ravine."

"It was flooded this morning." Hillary's voice rose with worry. "I passed it on my way here. My parents wanted to have Aiden over today but my Dad got the stomach bug, so I told Luke I'd watch him at home instead. And that's when Aiden got so mad."

Rainey couldn't discuss blame now, not when every moment counted. "Hillary, I've got to go. I'll call you if I find him."

"Oh, please. Please find him. Please."

It's you and me, God. I don't have a clue, so if You could give me a sign? A glimmer of what a little guy might be thinking? That would help.

She eased Spirit to a spot where she could see the ravine, but not risk the horse's weight on an eroded edge. The creek was swollen to three times its normal size, a rush of water cascading from the little falls above, streaming to the lake below.

Aiden wouldn't have gone there, would he? He loved the creek, he loved to roam the woods with his father, but would the danger of the water lure him? Or send him scurrying back uphill?

She didn't know, but she turned Spirit and urged him gently up the slope.

The rain had lessened. A hint of light to the west said the clouds were thinning, but the day was waning. Soon it would be dark. Too soon.

A sound drew her attention to the right.

She turned, scanning the woods.

Then the sound came again, farther uphill.

She spun back, astride the horse, and the sight unfolding before her made her heart stand still. A small doe leaped among the trees, dodging right, then left, her white tail flagging in the dank, dark woods. Behind her, a black bear gave chase, either hungry or mad, Rainey didn't know. Or care.

Because there to the left of the bear and deer stood a frightened five-year-old boy, drenched to the skin and afraid to move.

The deer pounded past Aiden.

So did the bear.

Then the deer leaped over the raging creek below, her dainty hoofs scrabbling in the mud on the opposite side.

The deer was safe, racing deeper into the woods beyond the stream, but failure didn't make the bear happy.

Rainey opened her mouth to warn Aiden not to move, but it was too late.

The boy spotted Spirit and started to race for the field.

The bear saw the movement and turned in pursuit. As Aiden streaked toward the cleared hillside, the bear assessed the boy's trajectory and dodged to cut him off.

"Get him, boy!" Rainey didn't have time to think. Going on instinct, she dug her heels into Spirit's sides and charged the bear.

Spirit responded as if he wasn't old or arthritic. As if he'd never spent a day lolling in a paddock with fresh green hay. Head down, he aimed for the bear as if he knew what was about to happen, and would risk anything to save Aiden. To save Luke's son.

The bear pulled up, surprised, but then aimed for Aiden again, curving upward, determined to take his prey.

Rainey didn't even have to move the reins. Spirit charged again, the slippery terrain making it hard to gain speed.

Rainey yelled with all her might, a battle cry that split the quiet of the remote countryside.

Her scream unnerved the bear.

She bellowed again, giving Spirit time to dig his way uphill, and as they drew closer the animal turned, judged the size of the charging steed and the crazed woman riding astride, and turned back toward the woods.

Spirit followed.

Rainey urged the horse past Aiden, determined to push the bear far into the forest. "Stay right there. Promise?"

The boy nodded and she let Spirit's pounding force drive the bear deep into the leafless trees, until she knew he wouldn't likely circle around.

"Whoa, boy. Whoa. Let's walk, okay?"

Spirit twitched his ears at the softened command. He slowed, then walked, ribs heaving, mouth open. She stopped him, dismounted, came around front and led him back to the meadow, where Aiden came racing toward them.

Spirit paused, catching his breath, and Rainey bent low to grab the little boy. She swooped him into her arms and held him tight, thanking God for his safe delivery. They stood like that for long moments, until a break in the clouds leaked sunshine onto the meadow.

The stream of warmth made Aiden shiver, and Rainey realized the boy had been wet and cold for too long. She pulled off her coat, peeled off her sweatshirt, then removed Aiden's coat and tugged her lined hoodie over his head. The dry, warm garment would insulate him better than a soaking wet jacket. She rolled up the long sleeves, then picked Aiden up, grateful beyond belief.

"Come on, kid, I'm putting you up top and we'll walk Spirit back home together." She boosted Aiden onto the big horse's back, made sure he held tight to the saddle horn and led the horse to the shoulder of the road. "It's not as steep here," she told the horse. She sent Aiden a smile and a wink, then led them both home.

Chapter Fifteen

Aiden was gone. Lost in the storm. And it was all Luke's fault.

What was the matter with him? He knew his son missed being with Rainey and the girls. He knew how well the boy had done since Rainey came back to town, and then Luke had separated the little guy from the first great experience he'd had since losing his mother.

Talk about dimwitted and shortsighted.

Luke's phone buzzed. He hit the cell button on his steering wheel and Seth's voice came through. "There's a major tree down on Town Line Road. Take Meagher's Hill Road to Log Cabin Road."

"That's five miles out of my way. Doesn't anyone have a chain saw handy?"

"Live wires. No options. Western Electric is on it, but they've got calls everywhere. Luckily, the storm's letting up."

It was. Luke saw the gradual brightening in the western sky, but he knew the outcome of such heavy rainfall in the mountains. Rushing streams and creeks doubled in size. Footing became treacherous. And if Aiden stayed on the road, he could be hit by a car, or a falling tree limb. Or stumble into live electrical wires. The host of traps awaiting his precious son put Luke's heart in a vise. How could this have happened? And at the worst possible time, when Luke was miles away, saving other people's homes. Other people's children.

Doing your job.

Luke pushed the internal voice aside. His job shouldn't take precedence over Aiden's safety. His—

A beam of sunlight broke through the thinning clouds, the shaft of light broken by the late-day angle and the lessening rain.

As Luke turned east onto Meagher's Hill Road, a rainbow blossomed over the rising hills before him, a splendid arc of promise and hope. And as he sped east, the colors deepened and spread, three-quarters of the arc back-shadowed by retreating clouds.

A rainbow.

God's promise to Noah, to his people. A symbol of hope and second chances.

Luke's heart cracked open, just a little. Was this a sign or just another scientific anomaly? He'd trusted God once, and God had failed him, utterly.

Was it God who failed you?

Or Martha?

Luke pinched the bridge of his nose, trying to thwart the rise of emotion, but the rainbow deepened as he drove, making him think.

You've carried her death with you for years. And her depression before that, thinking you weren't enough to make her happy, even though you tried. But maybe it wasn't you. Maybe it just was as it was.

Could it have been that simple? That Martha made a choice not because of who he was or wasn't, but because she'd felt powerless to choose otherwise? Maybe it wasn't all about him, after all. Maybe he wasn't a failure as a husband.

You loved her. She loved you. But sometimes love isn't enough. We need more.

God.

That's what his mother had counseled. That's what Rainey had said she'd pray for. For him to know the difference.

And the difference was God.

He stared at the rainbow, knowing God was infinite. He could watch over Aiden. Send him help. Give him shelter from the storm, as Isaiah had promised long ago.

Did Luke dare trust that?

He did the unthinkable. He pulled off onto the shoulder of the road, stopped the car, put his head in his hands and prayed. "I know I'm stupid, God. I get that. And I know You've probably been tempted to wash Your hands of me, but don't. Please. Watch my boy. My son. Put Your arms around him and keep him safe when I can't, like now. Hold him. Care for him. And teach me how to be a better father, God. A better man. Amen."

Luke sat back, shifted the car into gear, then paused, surprised.

A second rainbow outlined the first, lighter in shade and intensity, but there nonetheless. And as he drove toward the twin arches, they began to fade, the colors slipping away like quicksilver.

It didn't matter. He'd seen them. He understood the message therein, the promise of God's love.

As he turned up Log Cabin Road, twin Kirkwood police cruisers streamed by him, lights flashing, sirens blaring. Luke made out more flashing lights up ahead, at the crest of the hill, near his home, but as he drew near, something else caught his eye and his heart.

The cruisers pulled up a quarter mile short of his house. Two policemen climbed out, and as Luke pulled in behind them, he saw Rainey, holding Aiden, both wet and tear-streaked, but alive and unhurt. But then he looked beyond them, just uphill, to the large, prone figure of a fallen horse.

Spirit. Dead. Gone.

The old gelding lay quiet, his big roan head resting on soft green grass, his huge heart silenced forever.

"Daddy!"

Sorrow claimed Luke at the sight of his old friend, but hope surged forth when Aiden broke away from Rainey and raced to his side. "I'm sorry, Daddy! I'm sorry! I shouldn't have run away. I should have listened to Aunt Hillary and you, and I should have just stayed in our stupid old house with nothing to do, but I didn't and now Spirit's dead."

"Oh, Aiden." Luke clutched the boy to his heart, feeling the cold in his wet clothes, his chilled skin, the paths of grubby tears trekking down his little cheeks. "We'll talk about all that later. You're okay? You're all right? Nothing hurts?"

He pulled back, thrilled that his son was all right, but Aiden's next words made him haul in a deep breath.

"Rainey saved me. The bear was coming after me, but Rainey and Spirit chased him down. They scared him, Dad. And Rainey can holler really, really loud, like people in those old cowboy movies you see on TV."

"Can she?" He turned toward her now, his heart overflowing with gratitude.

With love.

While he'd been face-to-face with his past and God's future for him, God had sent Rainey to save his son's life.

Piper's words flooded back to him. *"She's always had a sacrificial nature. That's Rainey."*

Why had he thought loving her could ever be

wrong? Why hadn't he seen that loving her and God would be the best blessing of all?

She took a half step forward, and her face—her sweet, beautiful, Madonna-like face—showed immense sorrow. "I shouldn't have taken Spirit. I'm so sorry, Luke." She pointed toward the barns. "But he seemed insulted that I even thought of taking Star out instead. And now—"

"Hush. It's all right." Luke put his free arm around her and tried to draw her in, but she pulled back.

"I have to get home."

He understood. The emotions of the moment would make it easy to stay with him, and she held back purposely.

For now, he'd let her. For now they needed to see to Aiden and Spirit, to treat boy and horse with love and respect. But Rainey McKinney had a surprise coming her way, just in time for a blessed holiday season.

A holiday season he intended they spend together.

Chapter Sixteen

Rainey watched as a contingent of sheriff's deputies took their spots at the crest of the south-facing hill the next afternoon. Chins up, gazes tight, they aimed long guns into the air and fired.

The sound split the late November day, a tribute to a horse, brave and true. A former deputy, laid to rest on the knoll of deep green pasture.

Dorrie clung to one of Rainey's hands. Sonya held the other in a solemn grip, but then she started forward, excited. "Oh, Mommy! There's Aiden and Luke!"

Her cry drew Luke's attention. He spotted them and moved their way, Aiden trotting alongside. Sonya broke free, racing from their quiet corner at the edge of the woods, and barreled toward him. "Oh, Luke!" She grabbed him around the neck and gave his cheek a loud, smacking kiss as he held her. "I've missed you so much! And I'm so sorry that

Spirit died. Luke, I'll miss him so much. Why don't you come see us anymore?" she demanded.

"I was stupid," he explained, and both Sonya and Dorrie went round-eyed at his use of a very bad word. "But I'm smarter now and I'd like to come see you. If it's all right with your mom."

Rainey's heart churned. Sonya turned her way, hopeful.

Dorrie clutched her arm, expectant. "Of course it's all right, isn't it, Mommy? We love Aiden and Luke, don't we?"

"I know I love you guys," Aiden added, his round-eyed gaze sincere. "And I miss playing with you. And Rainey's cakes."

Luke stepped closer, close enough for Rainey to see the tiny points of light in his clear blue eyes. He held her gaze, then indicated the girls. "I can meet you all in church tomorrow. If that's all right with Mommy."

Her heart sped up.

She took charge of her emotions and reminded herself that anyone could go to church. A mere presence meant little. She knew that firsthand, so chose her words carefully. "I'd love to see you guys in church."

His smile softened. "I suspected as much. Rainey, I—"

A crowd of people began moving their way. Rainey grabbed Dorrie's hand, then reached for

Sonya's. "I need to get them to a birthday party for one of the girls in Dorrie's class. I promised I'd bring them here first—" her gaze wandered over the freshly turned earth and she couldn't hold back a sigh "—to say goodbye."

"Rain, I need to—"

"We'll talk tomorrow. Okay?"

The press of well-wishers drew closer, and the last thing Rainey wanted was to talk with people, listen to their praise. If she'd thought things through, Spirit would have stayed safe in his stall and Star would have ridden uphill with her. Her choice…

As if listening to a horse was something a normal person would do.

Cost the old horse his life.

People were calling her a hero. News accounts had been singing her praises.

They were wrong, so wrong. Spirit was the hero, and now he was gone.

She grabbed the girls' hands and ducked away before she got trapped in the crowd of sympathetic neighbors and friends. She would apologize tomorrow. Ask Luke's forgiveness. Her eyes strayed to the flower-strewn hillside as she pulled the car out onto the road, the blossoms a tribute to a life well spent. Life was all about choices. When would she start making the right ones?

Rainey sensed the attention aimed her way when she slipped into the beautifully decorated church the next morning. Deep green garlands looped from window to window. Wide red ribbons marked the upswing of each loop. Tiny white silk flowers were tucked beneath the bows, while clear twinkle lights lit the strands from within.

Tall, broad evergreens stood on either side of the sanctuary, and a smaller version stood in the narthex, a giving tree, filled with names of people who needed help this Christmas. She let each girl pick a paper angel from the tree, and she would use her small stash of money to take them shopping for the needed items. Teaching the girls to give to others meant a great deal to Rainey. Learning to do without while appreciating what they had was a valuable lesson.

As she settled her daughters with their matching books about the first Christmas, Uncle Berto stepped out of the pew so Luke and Aiden could slide in.

He'd come.

He'd promised, yes. She'd heard him. And she saw a warm light in his eyes, a light that seemed brighter than she remembered. But it was Christmastime. Everything seemed brighter at Christmas.

"May I?" Luke let Aiden wriggle in alongside Lucia and Dorrie, then opened the music issue to the number posted on the vintage oak board up front. "We're low on books, it seems, but you and I can share. Right?"

He turned his attention to her, his eyes bright

and trusting, filled with light, and his look said he'd come a long way from the doubt-filled man she'd left weeks ago.

Could that be possible?

With God, all things are possible.

Rainey believed that, but…

Luke's voice, deep and low, joined in the hymn of Advent. Berto's off-pitch bass chimed in from behind them. Lucia's deeply accented soprano rose to their right. And in the middle, the tall, blond sheriff's deputy sang with genuine warmth and gusto.

Hearing him, imagining the boy that used to sing these same songs, now a man, coming back to God.

Rainey's heart filled with a joyous song that had little to do with music.

Luke sent her flowers on Monday, two beautiful poinsettias, perfect for the farmhouse living room.

On Wednesday he stopped by with cheesecake from a Buffalo bakery, an unexpected treat that went a long way to winning the entire McKinney clan back over to his side.

Friday afternoon a Christmas tree arrived, a full, gorgeous Norway spruce, the deep green branches perfect for decorating. And on Saturday morning a note came, inviting Rainey and the girls to help him and Aiden decorate their home after church on Sunday.

"I have to work," Rainey declared as she read the

note in the dairy store. She purposely ignored the way her mother rolled her eyes. "Marly is studying for her finals."

"You don't, and you know it," Lucia retorted. "I will be here, and Noreen has offered to help, as well. We love having you around, but we do not need you tomorrow. Go and help this man who tries so hard now to show you his faith. His love."

Rainey sat down on a tall stool, angry with herself. "I can't. I killed his horse. I should have known better. I should have—"

"You saved my son's life."

Rainey turned, startled.

Luke stood just inside the store entrance, his sweet face dark with concern. "Rainey, you've given me so much. How can you not know that?"

His deep voice and gentle empathy drew the attention of some shoppers.

"Luke, I—"

"You answered a call for help with no thought to your own safety." He walked toward her, counting on his fingers as he moved, and more customers caught the drift of the sweet drama unfolding. "You fought your way through a wretched storm, saddled a horse and rode into a squall to save my son's life. How can you think I'd be anything other than grateful? On top of loving you beyond belief?"

"I…"

Their conversation had now drawn the interest

of most everyone in the dairy store, but Luke kept his eyes on her. Just her. "When you saw Aiden in danger, you and Spirit chased off a charging black bear, with no concern for your own safety."

Customers nodded, clearly impressed.

Lucia backed away slightly, but not before Rainey spotted the broad smile on her mother's face.

"You challenged me to meet God, and I did, Rain. On my way home that day, He reminded me of something I used to know. That while God watches over us, and loves us, people have the gift and responsibility of free will. I forgot that after Martha died." Luke reached out his hands to clasp hers. "I was so busy shouldering the blame for her death that I forgot to put it in God's hands. Only He can see the heart and soul."

Luke gave a slight smile and gripped her hands tighter. "Will you and the girls come and help us decorate the house for Christmas tomorrow? Please?"

How could she say no? She nodded agreement. "Yes, we'll come. Now go back to work. You're embarrassing me."

His grin made people laugh. "I'll consider my visit a success, then. And if a *tres leches* cake happens to come along with you ladies tomorrow, I can't say I'd mind."

Rainey laughed in turn. "I'll bring one. I promise."

"Good." He pressed a sweet, soft kiss to her

cheek, lingering there for just a moment. "I'll see you tomorrow."

"Yes."

The crowd whispered as he left, and Rainey felt heat stain her cheeks, but then Mrs. Thurgood stepped forward and grasped her hand. "God has a way of putting us in the right place at the right time, if we're smart enough to pay attention." She reached out and gave Rainey a hug. "I'd say you've been paying attention quite well."

"Thank you." Rainey whispered the words for the old woman to hear, but then straightened, righted her apron and pointed to the new cake cooler alongside the milk cooler. "But as sweet as all that was, if I don't get to the back room and drench more sponge cake, I'll be working all night."

The customers smiled, and as Rainey threaded her way through them to the back room, she sensed their genuine joy for her.

For her.

And it felt unbelievably good.

Chapter Seventeen

"It's not as bad as it looks." Rainey offered from the kitchen where she was decorating cookies with Dorrie, Sonya and Aiden.

"It's pretty bad," Luke replied. He scratched his brow, clearly in over his head, surrounded by reams of garland, lights and decorations in the living room. "I thought we'd have this done in no time," he called out, and Rainey's burst of laughter made him smile.

"With three five-year-olds? What were you thinking, Luke?"

"I guess I wasn't," he replied as he stepped into the kitchen. He took a deep breath. "Well, the roast smells great, and so do these cookies, but you—" he leaned in and took a deep breath near Rainey's neck "—smell marvelous."

"Try this one, Aiden." She handed his son a shaker of red-and-green sugar, then turned toward Luke, but his proximity unnerved her. He saw that and smiled, touched a hand to her cheek, then backed away slightly.

"You were saying?"

She paused, smiled up at him and thought of how impossible this day would have seemed a few weeks ago. But the shambles of a living room meant there was work to be done and not much time to do it. Five-year-olds had short attention spans. "I think we should concentrate on the porch today. If we get that done, the house will at least look festive from outside. And then we can put the candles in the windows...."

"I don't have candles for the windows," he told her.

She edged past him to the box she'd carried in. "You do now. Julia found these at a garage sale, and they're perfect for this house. Sonya, go easy on the sprinkles, honey. Save some for the next cookie."

"'Kay." Sonya eased up on the little plastic shaker, lips pursed, deep in concentration.

Dorrie was busily applying thick buttercream icing in unhealthy amounts to the pile of sugar cookie Christmas trees in front of her. Aiden's job was to sprinkle sugar "lights" on the freshly frosted trees.

There wasn't a clean surface to be seen in Luke's normally pristine kitchen, and it felt wonderful.

"May I see you for a minute, Rain?"

She sent the kids a skeptical look. "You want

me to leave them alone, armed with frosting and sprinkles?"

One look at his face and she knew exactly what he was thinking, so she set down a frosting bag and followed him into the disheveled living room. Piper and her mother had donated boxes of extra decorations. Jenny Campbell had done the same, and Luke had followed Rainey's directions and purchased garlands for the porch. But the antics of three children had ground progress to a halt.

And in spite of that, Rainey had never enjoyed a more perfect afternoon.

She scanned the messy room and smiled. "As soon as I'm done with cookies I'll help out here, okay?"

Luke looped his arms around her waist. Drew her in. "Promise?"

"Yes."

"Good. Rainey…" Whatever he was going to say became lost in a kiss, a lovely kiss that brushed aside worries about ornaments and garlands. It was a kiss of promise and hope. Luke drew back eventually and pulled her against his chest, holding her, hugging her, the beat of his strong, steady heart a sound she'd love to hear every day.

"I don't want today to end," she whispered.

She felt him smile, his lips pressed against her hair. "Me, either. But I can think of only one way to make that happen, Rain."

She leaned back and gazed into his beautiful blue eyes. "And that is?"

"Marry me. Us." He waved a hand toward the kitchen. "Make us a family of five. Or more." He added the last with a little smile. "There's always room for a cradle, isn't there?"

Her heart surged. A glimpse of the future opened before her, children laughing and playing, climbing trees, building forts, feeding a menagerie of rescued creatures along the way. A future she hadn't dreamed possible just became likely; it was a dream come true.

"If you need time—" Luke began, but Rainey hushed him with a hug and then a kiss.

"I've had time. Plenty of it. Too much these last few weeks, so yes, Luke. I'll marry you. And raise these children with you."

Squeals from the kitchen meant they should really go see what the trio was up to, but as long as the knife drawer was out of reach, Rainey wanted to claim a bit more time with Luke. Just Luke. "And maybe God will send these guys a little brother or sister. Or two."

Rainey reached up and cradled Luke's face in her hands. Such a big, rugged protector to have such a kind, gentle heart. She loved that about him, the odd balance. She loved…him. "Shall we tell the children?"

"Not yet." He stole one more kiss, a claim-staking kiss, then held out a tiny, black velvet box. "To seal the deal."

She laughed, opened the box and sighed.

"You like it?" Genuine worry deepened his voice, as if any woman wouldn't fall in love with the pretty ring inside.

"I love it, Luke."

He reached out and plucked the flawless round diamond from the jeweler's box and slid it on her finger. "You won't make me wait too long, will you?" Luke grinned.

She sent him a scolding look, then kissed him again, laughing. "Winter's my quiet time at the store. I think we can find time for a wedding in the snow."

"Mommy! Look! It's snowing outside!"

Three sticky five-year-olds raced to the front window, marveling at the first real snowfall. Eyes wide, they hurried into jackets and mittens and dashed outdoors, welcoming the new season.

Rainey smiled up at Luke. "You sure you're up for all this?"

He looped his arms around her and dropped his chin to her hair. "I couldn't be happier, Rain."

Her heart melted a little more. This man had gone through rough times. He'd tried to stand tough and firm on his own, until circumstances brought him back to God. She settled her cheek against his chest, the glow of colorful twinkle lights sparkling against the late-day snow, and whispered, "Me, either."

Epilogue

"You look like you could use some help," Luke observed as he walked through the McKinneys' side door the weekend before Christmas.

Rainey turned from a sea of cotton and terry cloth on the living room floor and frowned. "You think?"

Lucia headed his way from the kitchen, plunked a hefty sandwich down in front of him, said "Eat!" and crossed the dining room. "I will take care of Doralia's angel gown. You do Sonya. Then we will both tackle the boy."

Luke coughed to hide a laugh.

Rainey's dark look said he'd made the wise choice as she shifted Sonya to tie a blue satin ribbon around her waist.

"Do they have enough layers on?"

"Enough so they can barely walk," Rainey told him. "And it's only going down to the upper twenties, so they'll be fine. And I think you're supposed to be eating, not talking."

"The sheep can keep us warm." Sonya lifted wide, round eyes to the adults. "Just like in that book about the little lamb that couldn't walk right. I love that story so much. Every time I see Luke's sheep, I think of that little lamb."

"Me, too." Aiden offered an upside-down nod from the sofa. "He stayed near the baby to keep him warm. That was a real good idea."

"They have portable heaters hidden behind the props," Rainey reminded them. "And there are two fire pits with adult shepherds watching over them. So it will be chilly, but not too cold. And remember, the real Mary and Joseph didn't have heaters in Bethlehem, so we're very blessed."

"I second that," Luke said as he finished the sandwich. "Lucia, thank you, that was delicious. Would you like me to—"

"Nope." Rainey interrupted whatever offer he was about to make with a quick shake of her head. "You take this one." She steered Sonya in his direction. "She just needs the silver angel wings from that pile near the kitchen. I'll get Aiden ready."

"Dad, look at this!" Aiden jumped down to show off the long flannel robe they'd borrowed from Jack's youngest boy. "Shepherds get to take care of the sheep, just like I do at home!"

"Someone, perhaps, should warn the sheep," Lucia murmured.

Luke grinned as he gathered their first angel into

his arms. "I'll take Sonya to the car and then come back for angel number two."

Rainey nodded and put her palms on Aiden's shoulders, then met the excited boy's gaze. "Kid, if you don't stop wiggling, I'm either going to stab you with a pin or we'll miss our time spot at the Nativity. Hold still."

"Sorry." He peeked up at her, a little guilty and very cute, then threw his arms around her in a big hug that almost knocked her to the floor. "Thank you for letting me do this, Rainey."

The feel of the boy, trusting and happy, of his big, smacking kiss against her cheek, made her smile. "You're welcome. Now quit buttering me up and let me get this done." She buttoned the dark brown fleece robe over his blue jeans, turtleneck and flannel shirt, then took the gold-toned bath towel and dropped it over his head. Blond curls popped through the neck slit and she cinched the terry cloth with a length of plain rope. Warm boots took the place of old-world sandals because December nights in Western New York were not open-toe-friendly.

"I'm wearing a towel on my head?" Aiden's eyebrows shot up in a look so much like his father's that Rainey's heart went to putty on the spot.

"Shepherds get the warmest heads of all in an outdoor living Nativity," she told him. She folded the towel, laid it over his head, then used a long, narrow, ragged piece of cotton cloth to tie it in place, letting the ends drape down the little boy's back. Pleased, she stood, stepped away and grinned at him. "You are the best-looking shepherd I've ever seen, Aiden."

"Really?" Delight brightened his blue eyes.

"What about me, Mommy?"

Rainey turned as Luke came back into the house. "Dorrie, in spite of way too much arguing and fussing at your grandmother—"

Guilt flushed the little girl's cheeks.

"You look exactly like a little angel should. Slightly frazzled and a little askew."

"Huh?"

Luke laughed and picked her up to carry her to the car. "She means you're a kid. But you look great."

"Oh." Dorrie's expression said she was okay with that. "Is it still snowing?"

"Yes. And probably enough to go sledding tomorrow after church."

Dorrie pumped her fist in the air. "Our first sledding this year!"

By the time Luke returned for Aiden, Rainey and Lucia had bundled up. Uncle Berto brought the farm truck around to pick up Lucia, and they made a rolling convoy down the hill to the village church.

The historic town square carriage house had been converted to a Christmas stable. Animals nibbled hay in the fenced yard adjacent to the old garage. Portable spotlights lit up the timeless scene of Mary and Joseph, with bales of straw as a backdrop. Rustic beams hid overhead lighting, bathing shepherds and angels in a warm glow.

Cars pulled into the various village lots for the annual event—an Advent walk, caroling from church to church, dressing the church doors in festive greens, then ending in the village square, where the living Nativity took place.

"Mom, quit fussing, I'm fine." Dorrie sighed loudly and waved Rainey away as she tried to straighten Dorrie's sparkly wings one last time. "I bet the real angels' mothers didn't do this."

"Oh, I expect they did," drawled Luke, but he winked at Dorrie, grabbed Rainey's hand and drew her back, out of the scene. "Come with me."

"But—"

He shook his head and made her follow along. "You need to see this from up here before all the people come." He climbed the rise of the west-facing hill, just enough to give them a vantage point above Main Street and the square.

"Oh, Luke."

He settled his arms around her from behind and rested his chin on her hair. "Amazing, right?"

"Beyond that."

Before her lay the scene she'd dreamed of for three long years. Her daughters, dressed for Christmas, taking part in the long-time tradition of their church. Slightly crooked wings gleamed beneath the hidden lights above. Their faces shone as they perched on their "risers" behind Mary and Joseph. Shepherds of varying heights wandered the scene. And Aiden had done just what he'd promised: he'd nipped a lamb from the fenced yard. True to his word, he and the baby lamb sat alongside the manger, making sure the newborn king stayed warm.

"Happy?" Luke whispered the word against Rainey's ear and the warmth of his breath made her sigh.

"Way more than happy."

His smile tickled her cheek. "Good." He turned her slightly, captured a sweet Christmas kiss, then rested his cheek against hers for long, precious seconds. "Merry Christmas, Rainey."

It was the merriest of Christmases, she thought. She didn't need presents or garlands or anything other than what she had this quiet, snow-filled night. The grace of God, a wonderful man who shared her heart and her faith, and three healthy, beautiful children.

She had everything she'd ever hoped for, right here. Tonight. She turned toward him and stretched up for one more kiss, knowing one more could never be enough. "Merry Christmas, Luke."

* * * * *

Rainey Cabrera McKinney's Tres Leches Cake
(Three-Milk Cake)

Sponge cake:
1 cup all-purpose flour
6 eggs (3 will be separated, it sounds sad, but it's fine, I promise!!!)
1 cup sugar
2 teaspoons almond flavoring, if desired. (We love almond so we add it.)
2 large mixing bowls

In one bowl, put 3 eggs and 3 egg yolks. Add the sugar and flavoring (if used) and beat with mixer until pale yellow in color. This should take several minutes. In second bowl (making sure there's no grease on/in bowl) beat the 3 egg whites until stiff peaks form. Fold the whipped egg whites into the beaten egg/sugar mixture. Sift the cup of flour over the mix and fold in with spatula, just until flour streaks disappear. Don't overmix. We want the cake spongy and light, ready to receive the milk syrup later…. *Oh, yum….* Using a spatula, gently put the cake batter into a buttered 13" x 9" pan.

Bake at 325° on center rack until cake is puffy and golden. Sides should pull away from pan slightly. Once cake is removed from oven, allow to cool a few minutes, then flip cake onto large tray or plate with sides to prevent sauce from spilling over. Using a large fork or a steel knife sharpener (this is what Rainey and I prefer, those rounded steel rods that come with knife sets, perfect for poking holes!) poke holes at ½" intervals throughout cake. No, you don't need to measure the distance, just "guesstimate," okay? Nothing goes wrong if holes are closer.... You want that milk sauce to penetrate throughout the cake.

Milk Sauce:
Mix together in medium saucepan:
½ cup corn syrup
¾ cup evaporated milk
¾ cup sugar
Heat to boiling over medium heat, and then simmer about five minutes, until pale caramel/gold in color.

Mix in:
1 12 oz. can evaporated milk
²/₃ cup coconut milk (for coconut variety) or ²/₃ cup half-and-half or light cream (for regular recipe)

Mix together, then spoon over cake slowly, allowing syrup to drench cake.
1 can sweetened condensed milk can be used instead of first three ingredients, but if you don't have it on hand, the mix of sugar, corn syrup and evaporated

milk makes an amazing milk sauce and takes only minutes on top of the stove. It does bubble, so make sure pan is big enough that it doesn't overflow. If using the canned variety, no need to heat.

Refrigerate cake, then top with Whipped Cream: Whip 2 cups heavy whipping cream and ½ cup sugar until stiff peaks form. Spread over cooled cake. May be garnished with fruit, nuts, coconut, etc. Whatever you like! Keep refrigerated and this cake is even better on day two or three. But that rarely happens around here. J This great recipe has become a family favorite for the Hernes in Upstate New York—and now the McKinneys of Kirkwood Lake!

Dear Reader,

Rainey Cabrera's bad-girl past probably reflects someone we all know. In this heartfelt Christmas story, we glimpse the errant teen within the penitent and self-sacrificial woman who struggles to make amends for thoughtless youthful blunders.

It is easy for kids to go astray these days. Temptation lurks everywhere. And like the adulterous woman in the Bible, we see some of the Kirkwood locals shunning Rainey. Who better to match her with but one of the gorgeous Campbell boys? Brought up in a faith-filled, ethnically diverse family, Deputy Luke Campbell's guardian image was shattered by his wife's death. Putting this hard-working and overprotective single father into Rainey's "raise 'em strong" care bumps heads...and then hearts. In a story that flows from autumn's abundant harvest to the celebration of Christ's birth, we watch love unfold as it should, one sweet step at a time.

I love to hear from readers! You can visit me at ruthloganherne.com, stop by my blog at www.ruthysplace.com, email me at ruthy@ruthloganherne.com or hang out with a bunch of talented authors at www.seekerville.blogspot.com. Or you can snail mail me in care of Love Inspired Books, 233 Broadway, Suite 1001, New York, NY 10279.

Thank you so much for buying this book! Your

gift of time blesses me, and I pray that each of you will have a joyous and blessed holiday season. Merry Christmas!

Ruthy

Questions for Discussion

1. This story begins with parents who fear their kids are about to fail kindergarten. Do you think it's tougher for parents these days or are they focusing on the wrong things?

2. Luke's life turned upside down with his wife's death. He felt abandoned by God. In return, he brushed aside his faith, determined to make it on his own. Has life ever thrown you such a curveball that you struggled in your faith? What helped you?

3. Rainey's got a lot on her plate, but we see that her sacrificial nature was part of what got her into trouble as a teen. Maturity helps us recognize our flaws. Do you have regrets that have dogged you from childhood mistakes?

4. I love small towns! Having lived in one for forty years, I recognize the good and the bad in small-town living. What do you do to stay out of the quicksand of gossip?

5. Hillary Baxter is angry at the idea of Rainey in Luke's and Aiden's life. What can help extended family members deal with changing roles due

to death and/or divorce? How can we help that adjustment?

6. When Rainey's booth was damaged at the bicentennial festival, how easy would it have been for her to just turn tail and run? What would you have done in that situation?

7. Luke's mother walks a fine line of encouragement and advice, trying not to step over the line, but her approval of Aiden's improved behavior is notable. As a parent, can you talk frankly with your parents or grandparents about raising children? Do you have an available support group?

8. Rainey knows she is falling in love with Luke, but when she realizes that he's fallen away from his faith, reality sets in. Can she risk entering into a relationship with someone who doesn't share her faith in God? Have you ever had to make tough decisions rather than risk your faith?

9. Luke's moment of truth comes when he realizes that his child is facing danger and he can't get there in time. The example of Rainey's faith, his parents' encouragement and Luke's self-appraisal makes him realize that God is always with his child. Luke finally finds peace in the Lord. Do you find it difficult to hand over worry to God? Does it help?

10. Rainey rushes to rescue Aiden and chooses to saddle up the aged horse, Spirit. She saves the boy's life, but the horse loses his life. Luke tells her how grateful he is to her, that God put her in the right place at the right time. Have you ever felt that God has put you exactly where you need to be at times?

11. Having the children take part in a living Nativity was a perfect epilogue for this lovely Christmas book! Have you ever taken part in a living Nativity or helped organize a kids' Christmas pageant? Isn't their joy beautifully contagious?

LARGER-PRINT BOOKS!

GET 2 FREE LARGER-PRINT NOVELS PLUS 2 FREE MYSTERY GIFTS

Love Inspired

Larger-print novels are now available...

YES! Please send me 2 FREE LARGER-PRINT Love Inspired® novels and my 2 FREE mystery gifts (gifts are worth about $10). After receiving them, if I don't wish to receive any more books, I can return the shipping statement marked "cancel." If I don't cancel, I will receive 6 brand-new novels every month and be billed just $5.24 per book in the U.S. or $5.74 per book in Canada. That's a savings of at least 23% off the cover price. It's quite a bargain! Shipping and handling is just 50¢ per book in the U.S. and 75¢ per book in Canada.* I understand that accepting the 2 free books and gifts places me under no obligation to buy anything. I can always return a shipment and cancel at any time. Even if I never buy another book, the two free books and gifts are mine to keep forever.

122/322 IDN F49Y

Name	(PLEASE PRINT)	
Address		Apt. #
City	State/Prov.	Zip/Postal Code

Signature (if under 18, a parent or guardian must sign)

Mail to the **Harlequin® Reader Service:**
IN U.S.A.: P.O. Box 1867, Buffalo, NY 14240-1867
IN CANADA: P.O. Box 609, Fort Erie, Ontario L2A 5X3

**Are you a current subscriber to Love Inspired books
and want to receive the larger-print edition?
Call 1-800-873-8635 or visit www.ReaderService.com.**

* Terms and prices subject to change without notice. Prices do not include applicable taxes. Sales tax applicable in N.Y. Canadian residents will be charged applicable taxes. Offer not valid in Quebec. This offer is limited to one order per household. Not valid for current subscribers to Love Inspired Larger-Print books. All orders subject to credit approval. Credit or debit balances in a customer's account(s) may be offset by any other outstanding balance owed by or to the customer. Please allow 4 to 6 weeks for delivery. Offer available while quantities last.

Your Privacy—The Harlequin® Reader Service is committed to protecting your privacy. Our Privacy Policy is available online at www.ReaderService.com or upon request from the Harlequin Reader Service.

We make a portion of our mailing list available to reputable third parties that offer products we believe may interest you. If you prefer that we not exchange your name with third parties, or if you wish to clarify or modify your communication preferences, please visit us at www.ReaderService.com/consumerchoice or write to us at Harlequin Reader Service Preference Service, P.O. Box 9062, Buffalo, NY 14269. Include your complete name and address.

LILPDIR13R

LARGER-PRINT BOOKS!

GET 2 FREE
LARGER-PRINT NOVELS
PLUS 2 FREE
MYSTERY GIFTS

Love Inspired®
SUSPENSE
RIVETING INSPIRATIONAL ROMANCE

Larger-print novels are now available...

ReaderService.com

Manage your account online!

- Review your order history
- Manage your payments
- Update your address

**We've designed
the Harlequin® Reader Service
website just for you.**

Enjoy all the features!

- Reader excerpts from any series
- Respond to mailings and
  special monthly offers
- Discover new series available to you
- Browse the Bonus Bucks catalog
- Share your feedback

Visit us at:
ReaderService.com